מסורה

ArtScroll Youth Series®

Tales From Old Jerusalem

Tales from

by

Rabbi Shlomo Zalman Sonnenfeld

translated by David Kerschen
and Michael Elzufon

illustrated by Miriam Bardugo

Old Jerusalem

GREAT TALES ABOUT EVERYDAY PEOPLE
IN OLD JERUSALEM

Published by

Mesorah Publications, ltd

FIRST EDITION
First Impression . . . December, 1989

Published and Distributed by
MESORAH PUBLICATIONS, Ltd.
Brooklyn, New York 11232

Distributed in Israel by
MESORAH MAFITZIM / J. GROSSMAN
Rechov Harav Uziel 117
Jerusalem, Israel

Distributed in Europe by
J. LEHMANN HEBREW BOOKSELLERS
20 Cambridge Terrace
Gateshead, Tyne and Wear
England NE8 1RP

Distributed in Australia & New Zealand by
GOLD'S BOOK & GIFT CO.
36 William Street
Balaclava 3183, Vic., Australia

Distributed in South Africa by
KOLLEL BOOKSHOP
22 Muller Street
Yeoville 2198, South Africa

ARTSCROLL YOUTH SERIES®
TALES FROM OLD JERUSALEM
© *Copyright 1989, by* MESORAH PUBLICATIONS, Ltd.
4401 Second Avenue / Brooklyn, N.Y. 11232 / (718) 921-9000

ISBN:
0-89906-843-X (hard cover)
0-89906-844-8 (paperback)

Typography by CompuScribe at ArtScroll Studios, Ltd.
4401 Second Avenue / Brooklyn, N.Y. 11232 / (718) 921-9000

Printed in the United States of America by Noble Book Press Corp.
Bound by Sefercraft, Quality Bookbinders, Ltd. Brooklyn, N.Y.

Table of Contents

Publisher's Foreword

Rabbi Shlomo Zalman Sonnenfeld is familiar to ArtScroll readers from *Guardian of Jerusalem* — his masterful biography of his great-grandfather, Rabbi Yosef Chaim Sonnenfeld — and *Jerusalem Gems*, the forerunner of this book. He is a Talmudic scholar of note, a teacher with sensitivity and insight, a man who lived most of his life in the picturesque neighborhoods of Old Jerusalem, a political leader and city planner who is responsible for some of the new Jerusalem's most popular Orthodox neighborhoods and for preserving the holiness of the Holy City as it grows and expands.

Rabbi Sonnenfeld is a master storyteller who grew up with these stories and remembers some of the principals. The traditions and lore of the Old Yishuv were staples of the

Sonnenfeld household, a home of Torah, *yiras Shamayim*, and loyalty to the traditions of Jerusalem. When a man like Rabbi Shlomo Zalman Sonnenfeld tells about his city, the stories have unique flavor. We touch the personalities of the people and can almost feel the cobblestones under our feet. That is why we felt privileged to present his stories in *Jerusalem Gems,* and to follow up with this equally warm, wise and inspirational collection of *Tales from Old Jerusalem*. We echo his hope that a new generation of readers be moved by these tales of the spirit and that this book help Old Jerusalem remain ever fresh in the hearts of our people.

Rabbi Meir Zlotowitz / Rabbi Nosson Scherman

Preface

It is gratifying that *Jerusalem Gems*, my first book of stories about the Jerusalem of Yesteryear, was popular enough to justify a sequel. Clearly, there is a thirst for the purity and holiness, the aspiration and striving that characterized so much of Jewish life in the Holy City. Its rabbis and cobblers, its mothers and children were the shock troops of our nation, because they seized the privilege of living lives in which Torah and *mitzvos* were primary, and material comforts were unimportant. They saw the world a different, purer way, and that is a legacy that must be preserved as it is in these true stories.

In that volume, I tried to define the secret, the power concealed within these unforgettable tales of the Holy city.

King David ascribes נֵצַח, *triumph*, to G-d (*I Chronicles* 29:11). What is this "triumph," of which David speaks?

Rabbi Akiva teaches נֵצַח זוֹ יְרוּשָׁלַיִם, *"triumph" alludes to Jerusalem* (*Berachos* 8a).

Jerusalem is synonymous with triumph. Triumph is eternal,

undiluted, impervious to deterioration. This is the secret of Jerusalem's enduring charm. Anything relating to its lore and its people is vibrant and dynamic. In fact, Jerusalem is synonymous with life itself (*Avos d'Rabbi Nassan* 34:10); it is forever attached to its celestial counterpart.

So it was in the past and so it is now. The intoxicating ambiance of Jerusalem has not been weakened to this very day; it is incomparable. Like wine, the stories of Jerusalem deepen and improve with age.

These tales are in my veins, transfused into them by my parents and grandparents, and those who lived them. I have tried to present the facts as they occurred, flavored only by insights into the people as I knew them, or as their essence was conveyed to me. And I have tried to make the reader experience the same electric thrill I felt when I first heard them. The store of such tales is endless, but I have selected only those that have a moral lesson, so that new generations can absorb the greatness of their forebears. As we await the coming of the Redeemer, may it be soon, in our lifetime, let these stories remind us of the stature of those who laid the foundations for the spiritual triumph of the future.

❈   ❈   ❈

Once again, I express my gratitude to my dear friends Rabbi Meir Zlotowitz and Rabbi Nosson Scherman, who have made ArtScroll the leading publisher of Torah literature in English. As publishers of *Guardian of Jerusalem* and *Jerusalem Gems*, they have demonstrated dedication to excellence and the needs of *Klal Yisrael*.

Shlomo Zalman Sonnenfeld

Marcheshvan 5750
Jerusalem

Tales From
Old Jerusalem

The Fruit of a Beautiful Tree

R' Yaakov Meir Sonnenfeld, son of the great R' Yosef Chaim Sonnenfeld, never left the tent of Torah throughout his life. And his wife was a true helpmate for him. No sooner had he put down the *Havdalah* cup than she would urge him, "*Nu*! R' Yaakov Moshe (the *gaon* R' Yaakov Moshe Charlop) is already waiting for you. Hurry!" And with the departure of the *Shabbos*, he would make his way to his *chavrusa*, R' Yaakov Moshe, in one of the small synagogues of the city to return home only at the week's close on Friday afternoon. Their constant learning was broken by an occasional nap in the *ezras nashim*, the women's section of the *shul*.

With time, as his family grew, he moved from the little synagogue to the Chasam Sofer Yeshivah in the Batei Ungarin (Hungarian houses) neighborhood and became a member of its *kollel*. The meager allowance he received barely allowed him to make ends meet. Fortunately, he was satisfied with the least of the least; during the week he subsisted on dry bread, herring and a few olives. And his clothes, though spotless, were simple.

He had but one extravagance — the *esrog* for *Succos*. The Torah commands us to take 'the fruit of a beautiful tree' and that fruit itself needs to be beautiful. The measure of beauty is not given; there is no upper limit. But if beauty was the essence of the *mitzvah*, R' Yaakov Meir was ready and willing to give his all for a queen of an *esrog*.

Each year he sought and he found. His *esrog* would rise in a curve to its point like a tower, topped by its delicate *pitom*. The ridges and grooves would be well defined. It was free of mottling or any imperfection, without blemish in color or shape. His need and desire to fulfill this *mitzvah* in an outstanding way eventually led to his becoming an *esrog* merchant in the Holy City.

But in the beginning. . .

With the arrival of *Elul* the need for an *esrog* would begin to gnaw at him. He would note the comings and goings of the local dealers who went off to gather *esrogim* in Shechem and the Arab villages of Kabu near Batir (the original Betar), and Um el Faham near Chadera. Unlike most of the *esrogim* grown in Jewish orchards, which were hybrids (from the *esrog* crossed with the lemon), those from the Arab locales had been considered for many generations to be of unmixed strain. And it was the pure *esrog* that was most sought after.

The merchants would return and R' Yaakov would be waiting. He would stand by a dealer as he sorted the fruits, and graded them, and wrapped each one like a jewel in its soft cocoon. When his sharp eye spied a promising specimen, he would dart forth and ask to see it. Perhaps it was this year's heart's desire. Confronted with R' Yaakov Meir's enthusiasm, the merchant would sweep the *esrog* out of sight. That was to be saved for someone important. "When I have an *esrog* for R' Feivel Minsker and one for R' Tanchum Bialistoker and one for each of the other worthies, then you can have a look at what's left," he would say.

R' Yaakov Meir would swallow his embarrassment and slink off to haunt a second, and then a third dealer, until he finally found his treasure, always at a top price.

But one year he was not so fortunate. It was a year of drought. The thirsty trees were bare, their leaves wilted. The few *esrogim* that ripened were not much to look at. Even a mediocre *esrog* was a precious find and they barely reached the market, only to be snapped up by men of influence and wealth, to whom price was no obstacle and with whom R' Yaakov Meir could not compete.

In the aftermath of that *Succos* Festival an idea took root and blossomed. "Why," thought R' Yaakov Meir, "should I rely on the offices and good will of the *esrog* dealers? Are they the only ones to whom the villagers of Kabu and Um el Faham would sell their goods? Certainly not! The farmers have eyes only for their profits. I will add a trifling sum to the price and I myself will buy a few crates of *esrogim*. With the best of the lot I will fulfill the *mitzvah* and the rest I will sell."

Towards the end of the summer, he approached the *gemach* (free-loan society) of Sha'arei Zedek, borrowed a few golden napoleons (the hard currency of the day) and, shortly before *Rosh Chodesh Elul*, he boarded the train for Yaffo. He got off at Batir and made his way on foot to the village of Kabu.

The cunning *fellahin*, seeing a new greenhorn dealer, scented a fine profit in the offing and tried to overcharge him. But they soon learned that R' Yaakov Meir was hardly a run-of-the-mill novice; he knew *esrogim* and their market value, and he came away with several crates for which he paid a reasonable price. Most of his purchases were *esrogim* of fair quality, some were superior and he had even managed to pick a few very special ones.

On *Rosh Chodesh Elul*, the formal beginning of the *esrog* season, R' Yonah Hershler, a veteran dealer, arrived in the village. He made a circuit of the orchards; his eyes bulged and his jaw dropped in shocked disbelief. In a choked cry, he barely managed to express his amazement. "What happened?" he said. "Where are the 'clean' *esrogim*?" The orchard owner was reluctant to reveal that a new Jewish hand had made the first pickings. He shrugged his shoulders, lifted his arms, and murmured quietly, "From Allah, *ya chavayah*."

On the first day of *Succos*, R' Yonah saw several of his old customers with beautiful *esrogim*. They had been purchased elsewhere and at lower prices than he had demanded. R' Yaakov Meir had stolen a march on the *esrog* market.

That first year R' Yaakov Meir's profit was the money he saved in not purchasing his *esrog* elsewhere. But with time, his business grew, until he became a major source for the non-hybrid *esrog*, *kasher lemehadrin* — kosher, beyond a shadow of doubt.

His was not the usual business establishment. He had a basement in Batei Natan, right off Meah Shearim, where he produced wine. And here he set aside a corner for the crates of *esrogim*. It was in this cellar and its adjoining courtyard that he would sell *esrogim* for the six weeks from *Rosh Chodesh Elul* to *Erev Succos*, from early morning to late at night.

For all his honesty, there was no shrewder dealer in the business. He had a knack for matching an *esrog* to the individual taste of each of his customers. This one liked an *esrog* with exaggerated ridges and grooves; that one preferred one with a 'gartel' — a belt around its waist. For the tall man he would suggest an esrog like a rising tapered tower; a round one for the plump man.

Unlike the other dealers, he never quoted a price directly. He would give it in a simple cipher, a gematriya, where the sum of the numerical value of the Hebrew letters of a word stood for the cost of the esrog. "For this fine one," he would say, "nothing less than chai (life = eighteen), or tov (good = seventeen) for one this good!" The customer might respond with a gematriya of his own: "Make it yud gimel middos (thirteen traits — referring to the attributes of G-d)."

But the esrog business was always incidental. R' Yaakov Meir made learning of Torah his profession. And in order to regain time lost from study after the six-week esrog season, he would throw himself into the sea of Talmud and Torah with renewed zeal for the remainder of the year.

R' Yaakov enjoyed his modest prosperity until the outbreak of World War I. With war came diseases — typhus, cholera, malaria — leaving death in their wake. And in 5676 (1916) a moving death attacked. A plague of locusts befell Eretz Yisrael, stripping the orchards and the fields bare. All was desolate and famine struck the land.

R' Yaakov Meir and his family shared the common suffering of all. But over and above the hunger and the sickness, R' Yaakov Meir suffered in his soul. Most of Elul had passed and hardly an esrog was to be seen; it was doubtful if one could make a brachah on the single one in his possession. How could one celebrate Succos without a proper esrog?

Rosh Hashanah came and went and still there were no esrogim to speak of. Immediately after Tzom (the Fast of) Gedaliah, R' Yaakov Meir set out on foot for Um el Faham by way of Wadi Arava and Wadi Kelt. The village was famous for its *esrogim*. But the villagers greeted him sadly. "The great Allah has punished us severely," they said. "He sent the locusts. Nothing is left in the orchards and fields. There is nothing to see." But R' Yaakov Meir begged them to take him to the orchard.

He went from tree to tree; he looked from branch to branch, praying for a miracle. And there was a miracle!

Hidden in the bush stood a tree saved from the locusts. It was wrapped in green foliage and among the thorny branches shone the lovely *esrogim*. One was fully matured, crowned in its glory by its *pitom*, still covered by leaves and surrounded, as if by a fence, by thorns — a detail of bodyguards assigned to protect it from the slightest harm. It seemed to say, "Here I am, waiting for you. Pick me and make a blessing over me. Let us rejoice on the seven days of *Succos* as the Torah commands."

The Arab villager saw in this a miracle from Allah and at first refused payment. But the glitter of the gold napoleons was too exciting and he, finally, succumbed and accepted them.

R' Yaakov carefully wrapped each precious *esrog*, placed them in his basket — one did not think in cratefuls that year — and started back for Jerusalem. His spirit sailed aloft and his heart full of gratitude for the *chesed* (kindness) that *Hashem* had shown him. He felt sure that the beautiful *esrog* was a sign — a sign of a year that would be free of troubles.

✑§ Partners

R' Yaakov Meir had reached the Holy City. He was anxious to visit his saintly father, R' Yosef Chaim Sonnenfeld, and tell him the tale.

His father listened to the excited retelling of the story of the miracle and gazed upon the lovely *esrog* which R' Yaakov Meir had taken from its bed with trembling fingers.

"Did *Hashem* provide you with only one such *esrog*?" asked R' Yosef Chaim.

"I did bring back several more, but. . .but. . .," stammered the son. Should he keep the *esrog* that he had gained by a miracle after trial and toil? Should he honor his great father and bestow it upon him? Was he permitted to turn his back, no matter what the cause, on this gift from Heaven? His confusion showed clearly on his face

His father understood his dilemma and waited patiently for him to solve it.

"Father," he said, "This miracle did not happen on my account, but through your merit. My joy will not be complete if your *esrog* were not a perfect one. I want you to have this one. But, if you agree, I would like to give it to you with a condition attached to it. Let us have a partnership. You will have a share in the *mitzvah* of my *esrog* and I will have a share in yours."

"Fine!" said R' Yosef Chaim, "I agree to the partnership, but I would like to benefit even more from our joint undertaking. You fulfilled the *mitzvah* of honoring your father and have stood firm in the face of temptation. I would like to share in that."

"The *mishnah*," said R' Yaakov Meir, "tells us that the principal of the *mitzvah* of honoring a father and mother remains intact for the World-to-Come, whereas a man enjoys its immediate benefits in this world. Let us, indeed, share. I will enjoy the immediate profits and you can have the principal."

"My son, if your heart is wise, my heart, too, will rejoice," (*Mishlei* 23:15,) quoted R' Yosef Chaim, beaming with pride. "Agreed!" And he placed the *esrog* in its place of honor, in his silver box; his son picked up the basket of *esrogim* and left for home.

On *erev Succos* while he was decorating his *succah*, R' Yaakov Meir received a messenger. "Your father has instructed me," he said, "to inform you that you should claim that which is yours; that he who puts his life in danger to perform a *mitzvah* with all his body and soul has earned that *mitzvah*. The agreement stands, but he wishes to pronounce the blessing over his *esrog* while you do so over yours. Both of you, as agreed, will share the rewards of the *mitzvah*."

And with that he handed the lovely *esrog* to R' Yaakov Meir. He had found the *esrog* and now it was his to keep.

And the Shabbos
Shall Guard You

O ne of the great redeemers of land in *Eretz Yisrael* in
the second half of the last century was a
Yerushalmi Jew by the name of R' Yosef Levi Chagiz. It
was he, who, together with R' Baruch Hirschnof, acquired the
land of the neighborhood of Mekor Baruch, now in the heart of
Jerusalem. Indeed, nearly every neighborhood established in
Jerusalem outside of the Old City walls, between 5655 (1895)
and the end of the century, was built on land that he helped buy
from the Arabs. He even bought five thousand *dunams* of land in
the western Galilee, around Teveryah and the present Kibbutz
Lavi, and planned to establish a settlement on it by the name of
Eretz Naftali.

R' Yosef Levi left no children behind. But the stories about him and his struggles to preserve the character of the Holy Land are the stuff of legends. They are his legacy to posterity.

R' Yosef Levi was as scrupulous about the seemingly minor *mitzvos* as of the major ones. But the *mitzvah* of *Shabbos*, in all its details, was especially dear to him. And just as he kept the *Shabbos*, the *Shabbos* guarded him.

He was one of the courageous warriors who fought against the desecration of *Shabbos* in the new *Yishuv,* in general, and in Tel Aviv, in particular. Many still remember the great proclamation displayed on the Blue House, which he owned, on Yehuda HaLevi Street, in the center of Tel Aviv. On it appeared in giant letters: *Zachor es yom haShabbos lekadsho — mechalleleha mos yumas* — (remember the Sabbath day and sanctify it — its desecraters must die).

The city of Tel Aviv brought him to trial in the British Mandatory Court for "posting a provocative sign without permission." He appeared before the British judge without a lawyer; he did not need one.

When the judge read out the charge, that in a proclamation posted on the front of his building he had fiercely cursed all who did not keep the *Shabbos*, R' Yosef Levi answered in a strong but calm voice, "I curse? The holy Torah curses them. If you do not believe in the Bible, you should bring suit against the Bible and not against me."

He won the case.

Aside from his real-estate dealings, R' Yosef Levi was involved in the production of paper and paper products. His factory was the first and biggest in Jerusalem. The second, in size, which was much smaller, belonged to the brothers Reuven and Ze'ev Zilberstein. R' Yosef Levi had inherited the factory from his father, R' Yitzchak, a great *talmid chacham*, as well as a sharp but honest businessman. The firm also had a branch in Yaffo.

With the advent of the first World War the economy broke down completely. The four years of the war, which had begun on *Tishah B'Av* 5674 (1914), impoverished the land and emptied it of everything. Throughout its duration, *Eretz Yisrael* was under siege by the British fleet and nothing could be brought in from the outside. Even local industry nearly ceased to exist.

In contrast, neighboring Egypt became the chief supply base for all the British forces in the Mediterranean Basin. Cairo, the Egyptian capital, became a center of military and economic activity, while the harbor of Alexandria served as the headquarters for the Royal Navy and Britain's allies.

What was true for the country was true for the paper business of R' Yosef Levi. The supplies which he had at the outbreak of the war became exhausted and were not replaced. Only in 5680 (1920), two years after the war, did trade revive. It was then that he decided to reestablish production in the Yaffo branch and made plans to travel to Cairo to purchase supplies. Somehow, his plans became known to the Zilberstein brothers and, in the way of the world of competitors, they, too, decided that one of them should go to Cairo for the same purpose.

Providence ordained that Reuven Zilberstein and R' Yosef Levi should share a compartment on the same train, as it made its way from Kantara on the Suez Canal to Cairo. It was a strained situation, since there had always been keen competition between the two men. But while sitting together, they made a mutual pact. If each were to individually approach the Egyptians, they would, immediately, sense the increased demand and raise their prices. The two Jews, therefore, agreed to place one order, as if for a single buyer, and afterwards mark the various packages indicating what belonged to whom.

Since the British military had top priority for the use of the train, it was very difficult to get a railroad car for civilian purposes. There was a long, complicated procedure and an extended wait before receiving authorization.

By spreading gifts and promising favors to various important people, the two paper manufacturers managed to get a freight car on the train that was to leave for Kantara the next *motzaei Shabbos*. However, they would have to see to the loading on Friday before *Shabbos*.

They shopped around for several days and found the quantity of goods required. An agent (*ra'is*) hired out fifty wagons to allow them to move their shipment to the loading platforms; they marked the various packages with their initials and decided on a central meeting place for all the wagons. From there, they would travel in a convoy to the train station.

On Friday morning, they began to gather their purchases together from the various quarters of the city. But Friday is the Moslem Sabbath. The Egyptians were slow in opening their establishments and loading the wagons. It was already two in the afternoon when the entire convoy was organized and ready to start for the train station. Reuven Zilberstein had a few more errands in town and he left the task of supervising the train-loading to R' Yosef Levi.

Finally, the convoy started on its way. After an hour or so of travel through the crowded Cairo streets, when they were not far from their goal, they found the road blocked by the military police. NO PASSAGE! A military supply line was coming from the station.

It was close to sundown and, even if normal traffic would be restored, it seemed that there would not be time to load all of the merchandise onto the train before *Shabbos*. And, indeed,

that became crystal clear shortly afterwards, when the street was reopened.

As the convoy approached the train station, R' Yosef Levi gave instructions to halt and not enter the station itself. The wagoners, their nerves frayed by the movements of the entire day, burst out with various threats; the *ra'is* quieted them with difficulty. When he was told of the need to avoid desecration of the *Shabbos*, he said that an immediate decision must be made, since the patience of the wagoners had run out.

"There is only one solution," said R' Yosef Levi. "Unload the goods onto the platform as quickly as possible; do not load them onto the train."

"Impossible!" said the *ra'is*. "It is illegal to use the platforms without prior permission. You have to unload from the wagons and load onto the train at one and the same time."

"Unload and load only the wagons bearing packages marked R.Z.," said R' Yosef Levi without hesitation. "As for the rest, the ones marked J.L.Ch., as far as I'm concerned, you can throw them straight into the Nile." He said this calmly. His soul was totally at peace with the loss. He would rather be a debtor for the rest of his life than risk desecration of the *Shabbos*.

"I am sorry to disappoint you, *Chavayah* Yosef," said the agent, "but I cannot fulfill your instructions. There is a heavy fine for dumping into the Nile, and most especially for such a large amount. Hurry! You do not have much time to think. The wagoners are restive and close to the bursting point. Then, all will be lost."

R' Yosef Levi raised his eyes to Heaven and said, "Master of the universe, whence cometh my help? Have I not, all my life, given of myself for the sake of Your holy *Shabbos*? Is it to be desecrated, now, on my account? Please do not put me to the test; it is too much for me."

And, then, he noticed, at the end of the street, a mansion surrounded by a fence. He asked the *ra'is* to wait a few moments and ran there. The fenced grounds were a huge lawn-like area with many kinds of shrubs and elaborate fountains shooting jets of water skyward. The gate was open and unattended.

R' Yosef Levi returned to the *ra'is* on the run and ordered him to lead all the wagons onto the nearby grounds and unload the goods in one corner of the spacious area. The *ra'is* followed his orders, not doubting that permission had been granted. The wagons entered in single file and the wagoners began the unloading.

While they were thus occupied, a splendid four-horse carriage entered the grounds of the estate. Within, sat a man of authority in a military uniform bedecked with ribbons and medals. There was no doubt who he was — the Governor-General of Cairo.

When he saw the strange activity, which had turned his private lawn into what resembled a freight yard, he asked his coachman to find out what it was all about. And a moment later, R' Yosef Levi was called before the governor to explain the "invasion."

In fluent Arabic, R' Yosef Levi explained what had happened; that he was ready to lose his goods provided that he would not transgress the *mitzvos* of *Hashem*; that pressure of time and lack of any alternative had not allowed him to seek permission to use the grounds and that he was willing to pay whatever storage fee would be demanded of him. He concluded by apologizing for his hasty action.

The stern countenance and the aloof manner of the governor melted and a forgiving smile took their place. The English soldier was filled with admiration for the man who stood before him, ready to lose his all, for a religious principle.

The governor thought a while and then said, "If I understand you correctly, you are ready to give up the entire contents of the wagons in order to maintain the sanctity of the Sabbath and the Divine command. That, to you, stands above any personal interest. If so, I suggest that you sign a declaration turning your property over to the state, since that is certainly preferable to throwing it into the depths of the Nile. The Bible, if I remember correctly, also, says that one should not destroy. If you will agree to this, then you will be forgiven for entering a military installation without permission."

"As for myself," said R' Yosef Levi, "I will agree without hesitation. But I have one request. Not all of the merchandise belongs to me; half of it belongs to Mr. Zilberstein. I transfer my part willingly, just as you ask. Perhaps, however, your excellency will agree to release Mr. Zilberstein's share."

The governor agreed and sent for his private secretary to draw up the declaration. At that moment there was not a happier man to be found than R' Yosef Levi.

While the secretary was preparing the draft, R' Yosef Levi supervised the unloading and, on its completion, paid each of the laborers his due. He, also, gave the *ra'is* an appropriate gift and sent them all away in peace.

He entered the governor's office in a state of spiritual exaltation. There, he was presented with the declaration. It was written on the official stationery of the Military High Command. Although it was in English, a language which R' Yosef Levi did not understand, he signed it without delay, not bothering to have it translated. He wished to show the governor that he fully trusted him.

He rose, apologizing that he had to return to his hotel, immediately, before the advent of *Shabbos* and he asked if he might leave his money and those objects which Jews are forbidden to carry about on *Shabbos* with the governor, until the holy day had passed.

"No need for that," came the reply. "I will see that you reach your hotel before the beginning of the Sabbath." The governor rang for his coachman and ordered him to take R' Yosef Levi to the hotel, immediately, in his official carriage. R' Yosef Levi thanked him from the bottom of his heart and, as he was leaving, the governor handed him a sealed envelope containing a copy of the declaration which he had just signed.

He arrived at the hotel before *Shabbos*, washed and changed. He was reluctant to pray in the synagogue near the hotel, because he did not want to meet Zilberstein. He was afraid that Zilberstein would press him and wish to find out what had happened in the train yards. And he did not want to talk about weekday matters on *Shabbos*. He was hoping to avoid Zilberstein until *Shabbos* was over, as they were staying in different hotels.

He still had no sense of loss. On the contrary, he had a wonderful feeling of deep spiritual satisfaction, because he had withstood such a severe test. And he spent the entire *Shabbos* in a high state of happiness.

After *Shabbos*, Zilberstein arrived, tense and upset. He had sought out R' Yosef Levi all day without success. He became furious when told what had happened and poured out buckets of abuse, shouting about excessive strictness and fanaticism. "We have lost our freight car," he cried, "and now it will be weeks before we get another. And there will be a fine for not having used the car allotted to us, and storage fees, and the price of lodgings, until we finally do get another car."

R' Yosef Levi restrained himself and did not answer. Did not the Talmud say: 'A man is not held responsible [for what he does] in his time of trouble'? Not everyone could stand up to the test; it was hardly right to be angry with him. For the sake of peace he merely said to him, "Zilberstein, you should be pleased. You still have your goods; I lost mine." And he showed him the copy of the declaration.

Zilberstein, who knew English, scanned the declaration and translated it for R' Yosef Levi. It read as follows:

The Honorable Mr. Yosef Levi Chagiz of Jerusalem is permitted by the military authorities to use any area on the mansion grounds for storage of an unlimited quantity of paper to be shipped to Palestine, until which time he shall obtain authorization from the train authorities for a car on which he will load the materials stored at the mansion.

The document was signed by the governor himself. Below the signature was an added note to the effect that Y.L. Chagiz obligated himself to remove his effects as soon as the train authority made this possible.

The contents of the so-called declaration were quite overwhelming. The governor, who believed in the Bible, had decided to test R' Yosef Levi's sincerity and he had acted out his scene to the end. R' Yosef Levi decided to continue the play.

The next morning, the two paper merchants paid the governor a visit and were received with great warmth. R' Yosef Levi, playing his part to the hilt, complained, "Now that the declaration has been translated for me, it is clear that the document does not reflect our agreement."

"*Chavayah* Chagiz," said the governor, grinning from ear to ear, "do you think I would stoop to take the property of a man who is ready to give it up for the principles of his faith? No praise is sufficient for such a man. His spirit is beyond praise. Had I the power, I would double your property. At least take my card; it will open the door of any government office in the city. And please turn to me if you are in any need of help."

They thanked the kind governor and parted from him in friendship, exchanging compliments in the Middle Eastern tradition.

From the governor's mansion, they made their way to the train station to clear up the matter of the freight car. On the way Zilberstein offered his apologies for his earlier anger. He had felt terrible and had been upset by the nightmare of expenses and losses which had been in store for them. But, now, he saw that a man who stands by his principles could very well win respect and admiration from those in authority.

As they approached, the stationmaster saw them from the window of his office. He rose and came towards them, waving a gold coin of ten pounds sterling in his hand. This raised their fears. He must be hinting at the fine they must pay for failing to use the freight car.

But there was another surprise in store.

"You must be worried about the freight car which you did not use," said the stationmaster. "Well, you have special luck; perhaps, that religion and faith of yours watched over you (apparently, the governor had already spoken to him). Friday afternoon, a textile merchant from Yaffo, who was slated to receive the use of a freight car this coming Tuesday, came to me begging for a car that day. He had to return home immediately, and he was willing to pay an extra ten pounds sterling for the change in schedule. I had the feeling that, as Jews who keep the Sabbath, you might not exercise your right to use the car. I told him to wait to close to sundown. An hour before sunset, when it was clear that you were not coming, I gave him the use of the car. Here is the extra money that he paid; it really belongs to you."

They refused to accept the coin, explaining that they did not wish to profit from maintaining a religious principle. But he insisted, maintaining that the freight car, and all profits from it, were theirs and theirs alone.

The story has a final twist. On *motzaei Shabbos*, the train bearing the textiles had left for Kantara. There it had stopped and the cars going on to *Eretz Yisrael* had been uncoupled. While they were being switched to another train, the last car, bearing the textile goods, had been disconnected and shunted off to a distant siding. Under cover of darkness, it had been rifled of its cargo.

On Tuesday, R' Yosef Levi and Reuven Zilberstein were allotted the car which had been reserved for the textile merchant who had not upheld the sanctity of the *Shabbos*. Everything was in order. They left Cairo thanking *Hashem* for the miracle which had occurred to them, calling it their 'Exodus from Egypt.'

Guardian of Shabbos

O f the ten measures of troubles that descended on *Eretz Yisrael* during World War I, Jerusalem received nine. Famine, disease and other woes reduced her Jewish population from fifty thousand, at the beginning of the war, to twenty-five thousand at its end.

In the first year of the war, business came to a standstill; each day proved worse than the previous one. Even the paper business of R' Yosef Levi Chagiz, one of the city's flourishing establishments, closed down. There were no printers and no other buyers of any sort; everybody was too busy trying to ward off his hunger and that of his family. Who needed paper when bread was scarce?

And so, R' Yosef Levi and his wife moved to Yaffo, the chief port of *Eretz Yisrael*, where the economy was still relatively stable, compared to Jerusalem. R' Yosef Levi had a branch of his business there. But not many days passed before that branch closed its doors, too. And then, R' Yosef Levi occupied himself with his orange grove in Petach Tikvah.

Aside from food, the most sought-after commodity was fuel, which, at that time, meant, chiefly, kerosene. It was imported in twenty-liter jugs, packed two to a wooden chest and was used for cooking and as fuel for lamps. The electric light was part and parcel of the fairy tales of tourists from the lands of the Diaspora, tales which excited the imaginations of the inhabitants of *Eretz Yisrael*, their eyes watery from the soot and smoke of the kerosene lamps.

Since kerosene was in such demand, there was a rash of hoarding of the precious liquid. Consequently the authorities announced that any man found with more kerosene in his possession than was reasonable for daily use would be punished with all the severity of the law and would even face the death penalty.

R' Yosef Levi, a man with a keen business sense, had realized at the beginning of the war that with the near-stoppage of imports, kerosene would become scarce. With an eye to the future, he had bought a considerable number of chests and hid them at the bottom of the well in his orange grove.

One *Shabbos*, to the surprise of the Arab watchman, a company of Turkish soldiers, under the command of a *kanon-javish* (major), entered the grove and conducted a thorough search. One of the men discovered the cache of kerosene in the well. The watchman, knowing well what was in store for his employer, paled.

The Turkish officer turned murderous eyes on the Arab. "What's this? Where is the *effendi* who owns this orchard?" he roared.

The watchman, all but struck dumb with fright, managed to stammer, "He lives in Yaffo and comes by a few times a week."

"Up on your horse and ride there as fast as you can! Tell him that he is to come and appear before me, *kanon-javish* of the Ottoman Empire. If he does not, his end will be a bitter one."

"*Ya'ami, ya-sidi*," said the watchman, "the *effendi* is a Jew and he will not come on *Shabbos*. Jews are forbidden to ride on their Sabbath day."

His words stoked the officer's anger. "Bring him here immediately! If he refuses, I will personally see that he comes. No man has yet dared to disobey an order of a Turkish officer!"

The watchman saddled his horse and set out for Yaffo at a breakneck gallop. After a ride of several hours, he reached the Neve Tzedek neighborhood and found R' Yosef Levi at his *Shabbos* table, peacefully singing *zemiros*. Trembling with fear, he told about the discovery of the kerosene and reported on the order of the officer.

R' Yosef Levi showed no sign of alarm. He finished *zemiros* and calmly recited *Bircas Hamazon*, the after-the-meal blessing. He then turned to the Arab and said, "First of all, tie the horse to the tree in the courtyard. Who gave you permission to ride him on *Shabbos*? Haven't I told you, time and again, that by Jewish law my horse, too, is required to rest on *Shabbos*? Get yourself a horse at a livery stable and return to the *kanon-javish*. Tell him that today is *Shabbos* and the command of G-d takes precedence over that of a Turkish officer. I'm sure he will understand."

"I told the officer that you would not come, but he could not imagine such a possibility. I see that I was right. *Chavayah Yussef*, have you for a moment thought of what this means?

There is no limit to the capriciousness of Turkish officers. To hang a man means nothing to them."

"He who fears G-d does not fear a Turkish officer," answered R' Yosef Levi.

The watchman tied the horse to the fig tree and went out to hire another animal, and soon was riding back to the orange grove. When he returned alone, without R' Yosef Levi, the officer was furious. He raved and ranted. "Where is the *effendi*?" he shouted.

"Didn't I tell you, *ya-sidi*," said the Arab, "that this Jew will not violate his Sabbath and will not obey any order that forces him to violate any precept of his religion?"

The officer assigned two men to stand guard over the well and swept off with the rest of the company. The following morning on Sunday, they returned. And on that morning, R' Yosef Levi rode his horse into the orange grove and presented himself.

"Why didn't you come yesterday when I summoned you?" said the officer. "Do you realize what is in store for you because of your disobedience?"

"I have been given counter orders by a higher authority," answered R' Yosef Levi.

"Who countermanded my order?"

"The great G-d!"

"G-d commands us all to obey the government. Were this not so, everyone would do as he wishes and say that he is obedient to G-d's demands."

"Certainly we must obey the government. But if your honor, the *kanon-javish*, received an order from His Magnificent Highness, the Sultan, may his glory increase, and your immediate superior would command you to do otherwise, whom would you obey? Do you not believe that our first obligation is to the King of kings Who reigns over us all?"

"Fine! And what about the kerosene lying in the well? Has your G-d also commanded you to put it there?" asked the officer.

"Absolutely!" answered R' Yosef Levi. "Do you think for a moment that I would endanger my life hoarding kerosene for myself? I set it aside for the poor with large families; those who do not have fuel to cook food for their children. You can ask in Yaffo and Jerusalem if *Chavayah* Chagiz lives for himself or the poor."

"But you are breaking the law and are liable to severe punishment, even hanging."

"G-d protects him who worries about the poor. And if you will help me aid them in their need, G-d will also protect you. Even in normal times we are all dependent on His protection, how much more so in these days of bloodshed."

A slight smile appeared on the lips of the hardened officer. "I myself am religious," he said. "I believe in G-d and I honor believers. Had you come yesterday and said what you just said, I would not have believed a word. There are many who commit every crime in the world and hide behind the name of G-d. But I have seen that you truly believe in G-d and are even ready to endanger your life not to violate His commandments. I am convinced that you are an honest man, and all that you say is true, as G-d is true. I will not arrest you; you are free! Take your kerosene and help the needy whom G-d wants us to help."

He barked an order. His men jumped to attention, saluted and marched smartly off. R' Yosef stood there, stunned and moved.

And the kerosene? Since he had said that it had been meant for the poor, R' Yosef Levi distributed it to the needy and their institutions. Not one jug did he keep for himself.

Saba Shmulik —
Every Child's Grandfather

For the thousands who studied at the Eitz Chaim Yeshivah in Jerusalem, the name Shmulik brings to mind sweet memories. For Shmulik was the friend of everyone at the *yeshivah;* he stood by each little boy the day he passed over the threshold to start *cheder*, until years later when he left as a mature *talmid chacham*.

Shmulik. Where did he come from? From which exile did he return? He was too humble and shy to speak of himself and his family. And no one else knew.

His manner of dress added to the mystery. The red turban and wide pants flapping in the wind reminded one of the Jews of the Orient. His shoes were unique. They were hand sewn and their rubber soles were cut from an old tire. Shmulik and his costume were a familiar sight. Often as not, he could be found rushing on an errand of mercy for some needy soul. And yet often enough, he could be seen slowly crossing the courtyards of Eitz Chaim, lost in the thoughts of a world of his own. Despite his bizarre appearance, Shmulik was so unassuming that he blended into the scenery of Jerusalem.

Shmulik subsisted on the minimum of food. His main meal consisted of dried *pita* (the flat bread of the Middle East) and a few olives.

His apartment, if such quarters deserve that name, was a single room in the old Churva courtyard, dating back to the days of R' Yehudah HeChasid. It had previously served as a study for the saintly rabbi of Jerusalem, R' Shmuel Salant. R' Shmuel's own two-room apartment had been as busy as a thoroughfare. Besides being his family's home, it had done duty as Jerusalem's *beis din* (rabbinical court), secretariat, assembly room of *talmidei chachamim* and, in times of need, a shelter for the poor. When the community saw how little privacy their beloved rabbi had, they set aside a room, so that R' Shmuel could continue to study and write in peace. When he passed away, Shmulik inherited this small room.

He did not need anything larger. No one knew if he had ever been married; he had come to Jerusalem alone. And he had not brought much of anything with him. A slab of wood was his bed, an overturned crate was a table and a rusty *chatzuvah* (tripod) served as his closet.

Shmulik did not know the pain of raising children. But the agony of being childless is far more painful. Yet, instead of nursing his hurt, Shmulik adopted the children of Eitz Chaim and gave them little treats which no parent or teacher could ever match.

And they loved him. A visit to his room was the highest of pleasures. His modest home was a little clubhouse where mischievous little boys gathered to hear exciting tall tales, which only Shmulek could tell.

But his room was more than a place of entertainment. It was a refuge in time of trouble or pain. If a child was thrown out of class, where else could he turn for help? Who came to his rescue and talked to the angry teacher? Who other than Shmulik for whom they were all "*mein kinderlach*" (my children).

And they in turn would do anything for him. They would fight to sweep his room, to bring him cold water from the well, to clean his red turban. And most of all they loved to stroke his long gray beard, while they sat with rapt attention listening to the far-fetched tales.

There was, however, one particular corner of Shmulik's room which was out of bounds. It was set off by a curtain and no child would dare venture beyond that curtain. For, besides being the *shammash* of the *yeshivah*, Shmulik was a member of the *chevrah kadishah* (the burial committee). And in that corner he kept the implements for the *taharah* (cleansing) of those who had just died. When Shmulik received notice of a death, he would lift the curtain, reach in and take out the dreaded instruments. He would balance them on his head and, with two pitchers tucked under his arms, would set off on his mournful task. Whenever the children would see him bent on such a mission, they would scatter before him, at once. Of course, there was always the impudent rascal who would approach and ask with bravado, "*Nu*, Shmulik, who died?" to which the aged Shmulik answered, "*Mein zeide* (my grandfather)."

"Much work and little blessing." How well that saying fit Shmulik. He performed many tasks, but received very little in return.

He was the shoemaker for the barefooted children of Jerusalem. How does one fashion shoes with neither hammer or nails? Shmulik knew how! He would shape the old piece of leather and wrap it around the tender foot. An old tire, some string, two hands and a kind heart went a long way in the Jerusalem of then. For ten *grush* (a small coin) the poorest family could buy a pair of "Shmulik's *shichlech* (shoes)."

He worked as a water carrier. For twenty *mils* (less than two cents) Shmulik would draw water from one of the three wells in the Churva courtyard and drag a twenty-liter earthenware bucket back to its owner.

Often a youngster would tease him, "Shmulik, whom are you working for? What are you going to do with all the money you make?" But Shmulik's only answer was a patient loving smile.

He saved the pittances he earned and placed each coin under a loose floor tile. Little by little, the sum would grow. And when he thought the time had come, Shmulik would remove the *mils,* the *grushim*, the half pounds and the pounds, and prepare for a journey to the Diskin Orphanage.

He would rise early, tuck the old leather pouch bearing his hard-earned money into his pants, and set out for the New City, outside the walls, while the morning air was still chilly. When he reached the entrance to Jerusalem, he would see the Diskin Orphanage on the neighboring hill. Up he would go, until he reached the fortress-like building and, still panting from the trip, he made his way directly to the treasurer's office. He would empty the pouch onto the desk. "These are my earnings," he would say. "I worked and sweated for the orphans of Israel. Now, please count the money and give me a receipt."

R' Yudel Shechter, the treasurer, would recruit two volunteers to sort and count the pile of copper and silver coins.

On one occasion, the final sum was one hundred and twenty-seven *liros* (pounds) and seven hundred and forty *mils*.

The act of writing a receipt is not a complicated one, but Shmulik had a special request. He would remind R' Yudel, "Don't write *liros* on the receipt. Write 127,740 *mils*. They represent the 6,387 buckets of water I carried on my back so that my precious children will be able to study and become *talmidei chachamim* and not simple water carriers like myself." There was no arguing with Shmulik. R' Yudel smiled and wrote, just as Shmulik had asked.

Shmulik was never upset or angry. But even for him there was a bitter day.

Shortly before *Succos*, one year, Shmulik, while crossing HaYehudim Street, noticed one of the boys teasing a retarded child. The ugly sight was a stab in the heart of the kindly old man. "How can a *ben yeshivah* (a *yeshivah* student) behave so cruelly?" he shouted. "If you do not stop, I don't want to see you in my room, ever again." His words fell on deaf ears. With a smirk on his face, the boy continued to harass the pathetic child.

Chutzpah — that mixture of disrespect and impertinence — was, also, a part of the tormentor's make-up. For, on the following morning, he walked into Shmulik's room as though nothing had happened. Shmulik was unable to control his anger and chased the troublemaker out. The youngster left the room both humiliated and enraged. His childish pride had been trodden upon and he dreamt of sweet revenge. He would bide his time and then. . .

Shmulik loved the *mitzvah* of *succah*. And each year, after *Yom Kippur*, during the four days before *Succos*, Shmulik would put his *succah* together. He insisted on doing everything with his own two hands — the walls, the *schach*, even the decorations. No matter how hard his little friends would plead, Shmulik

would accept no help. "I want full credit for this *mitzvah*," he would tell the children who gathered around to watch. And only when the last colorful sheet and the last decorative fruit had been hung would he rest from his work. His young friends would look and listen with open eyes and ears as he whispered his little prayer, "May *Hashem* grant me long life so that, someday, I will sit in the *succah* made of the hide of the *livyasan*!"

Shmulik found the task of erecting the *succah* more difficult with each passing year and that year it had been exceptionally exhausting. The picture of the struggling old man inspired the troublemaker whom Shmulik had driven from the room. One night of *Chol HaMoed* the miscreant and three of his cronies sneaked into Shmulik's *succah*. There lay the old man snoring gently. Each boy took hold of a corner timber, uprooted it and, in one swift motion, they carried the *succah* to a distant rooftop on HaYehudim Street. Shmulik had not made a move; he slept like a baby under the starry sky of Jerusalem.

At the call of the rooster, Shmulik awoke. He could not believe his eyes. Where was his *succah*, his *mitzvah*? Where did it disappear to? Did it fly to the heavens or sink into the earth? What kind of mischief was the devil playing? Who had committed this crime? In his entire life he had never slept out of the *succah*. Shmulik rose to wash his hands, the hot tears rolling down his cheeks.

The earliest arrivals of the *vasikin* (sunrise) *minyan* began to file into the Churva synagogue. They found Shmulik sitting hunched over on a stool in a distant corner, crying inconsolably. They all tried to comfort him but he would not be comforted. Everyone invited him to spend the holiday in his *succah*, but he flatly refused. He had never yet taken benefits from any man. "I will sit right here," he cried, "until my stolen *succah* is returned."

Among the visitors to the Churva that morning were the four

little thieves. They wanted to enjoy the sight of their victim's consternation. They sidled over to where Shmulik sat. They took one look — and froze. There he sat weeping his heart out. "Shmulik, why are you crying?" they asked in fright. Never had they seen a grown man cry.

"Why shouldn't I," he sobbed, "if this is what happens to me in my old age?"

"And if your *succah* is returned, what about those who took it, will you forgive them?"

"If they return my *succah*? Why, of course, I will forgive them. My little ones, please pray together with me that *Hashem* may forgive me for sleeping outside the *succah*." And Shmulik turned to pray, his plea punctuated with groans and wails.

The frightened little faces were white as snow. Finally, the ringleader mustered up courage and said, "Go, *Saba* Shmulik. Go, join the *minyan*. Soon they'll be up to *Krias Shema*. We promise you that when you return from *shul*, you'll find your *succah*."

And so it was. When Shmulik returned, there was his *succah* standing in its rightful place. The four little boys greeted their Shmulik with a bottle of wine. It was hard to tell who looked happier, the thieves or their victim. No questions were asked and no explanations were offered. Perhaps Shmulik knew, perhaps he didn't. But his deep wrinkles became even more pronounced as a huge smile creased his face. He opened his arms wide and gathered in his little friends and said, "*Kinderlach*, just as you helped me restore my *succah*, so, too, may we all together help rebuild *succas David hanofeles* (the fallen *succah* of David), our *Beis HaMikdash*."

R' Yaakov Galiner —
Rich and Righteous

In the early 1880's, a wealthy Jew in the prime of life moved from Poland to Jerusalem. His name was R' Yaakov Galiner.

R' Yaakov, a successful merchant in his home town of Galina, was exceptionally wealthy. He was blessed with fine children. Divine favor followed him in all that he attempted. He was well known for his generosity and his hand was open for every holy matter or public need. Yet, although R' Yaakov experienced only success, he was not pleased with his lot. His many ventures robbed him of the time that he would have liked to devote to the study of the Torah. All of his days, he strove to free himself from the bonds of business, in order to have the time to learn. But days turned into weeks, months into years and R' Yaakov remained submerged in the affairs of the world, while the question gnawed at his heart, "Torah, what will be of it?"

On the morning of his fiftieth birthday, R' Yaakov awoke with a verse from the Torah on his lips: "And from the age of fifty, he shall return from the ranks of service and serve no longer" (*Bamidbar* 8:25). He recalled the Talmud's statement that if one awakes with a verse on his lips, that is a small measure of prophecy (*Berachos* 55b). R' Yaakov saw this as a sign from Heaven; it was as though a voice from above had called out, "Until now you have worried about matters of this world. Now you must prepare for the World-to-Come!"

When R' Yaakov returned from *shul* that morning, he did not sit down to breakfast, as usual, with his wife, but went to his iron safe and took out a bundle of fifty one-hundred ruble notes. He summoned his wife Braina, handed her the money and said, "Here, take these fifty notes and distribute them among fifty poor people to celebrate my fiftieth birthday."

After breakfast, he told his wife that he had decided to retire and go up to *Eretz Yisrael*, in order to devote his remaining years to Torah and good deeds. R' Yaakov's good wife did not try to discourage him. On the contrary, she gave her full approval to the momentous decision. And so, though he then stood at the pinnacle of success, and his ventures all seemed destined to prosper, he liquidated his business, gathered together his money and made the journey to the Holy Land. There he settled in Jerusalem on Rechov (Street) Shalshelet, not far from the gate leading to the Temple grounds. And there, he found a large group of Sephardic and Ashkenazic Jews, almost all of whom were *yirei Shamayim* (G-d fearing) and who observed the Torah and its *mitzvos*. In short order, the successful merchant from Galina became one of Jerusalem's notables.

Within the walls of the Old City, R' Yaakov found peace. He had been accustomed to luxury and ease in Europe, while Jerusalem was then not much more than an abandoned ruin. But ease and luxury were not his goals. He sought to learn *Hashem's* Torah and the Jerusalem of those days was full of Torah and wisdom. *Tzaddikim* walked its alleys and occupied its *batei midrash*. R' Yaakov quickly found what he craved, the company of *talmidei chachamim* who gave their life over to the study of Torah, in the synagogue of R' Yeshaya Bardakai.

He made the great synagogue of Batei Machseh, where R' Yosef Sonnenfeld and R' Hirsch Michel Shapiro prayed, his permanent place of worship. In the presence of such great men, R' Yaakov felt spiritual elevation; all the desires of the world lost their meaning. Each morning, he would take part in the *vasikin* (sunrise) *minyan* and then stay on to learn until the third hour of the day (roughly, until 9:00 a.m.). In the afternoon, he would go to the Shoneh Halachos *shul* on Rechov HaYehudim and study until *Minchah*, after which he would hear the *shiur* given by R' Chiya David Spitzer to the working men of the community.

The *shiur* inspired R' Yaakov anew each day. It was well known that Jerusalem was a city of Torah giants and *tzaddikim*. But who would have ever thought that its tailors and cobblers, seemingly simple working people, were greater in their Torah wisdom than many rabbis abroad?

R' Gershon the smith, for example, hands still black with charcoal, had sat at the far end of the table arguing a fine point of the *halachah* and had displayed a complete mastery of the *Shulchan Aruch* and its commentaries. R' Yaakov had been abashed. For when this same R' Gershon had repaired his shutters, he had treated him as no more than a simple laborer.

Moreover, not only had he not shown him his proper honor, he had even haggled with him over the price. Who could imagine that one of Jerusalem's great *lamdanim* (Torah scholars) was masked by the work-worn face with its sooty furrows?

Once, R' Yaakov came back from *shul* deeply moved. "Braina," he said to his wife, "what I discovered today surpasses all I have seen to date. You remember R' Shaya Leib Blecher, don't you, the one who fixed the *Shabbos* kerosene lamp for us? He sits on the ground in a little wooden shack across from the Varshaver (Warsaw) *beis medrash*, hammer in hand, and never lifts his eyes from his anvil. He is a hidden *tzaddik*; he works from daybreak to dusk and never stops reciting *mishnayos* and *midrashei Chazal*. From evening to morning he studies Torah, taking no more than a brief nap. He sat at the table in the *shiur* in the Shoneh Halachos synagogue, his body bent from sitting constantly on the ground, his face aglow. R' Shmuel Schneider announced that we were to hear the considered opinion of R' Shaya Leib, 'whose heart is as wide as the entrance to an assembly hall.' R' Shaya Leib's humility shone forth as he gave his 'humble opinion,' as he called it. That 'humble opinion' settled the argument."

R' Nissan Schuster (shoemaker) did not repair shoes, he only made new ones. For were he to so much as handle old shoes, he would be unable to speak the words of Torah without washing his hands. And he did not want to stop learning for even a moment. No less an authority than R' Yehoshua Leib Diskin, the Rav of Brisk, had testified that R' Nissan was one of the *lamed vavniks*, the thirty-six righteous men found in each generation in whose merit the world continues to exist. When R' Yaakov heard this, he hid the shoes he had bought from R' Nissan in a closet; they were henceforth to be treated like a sacred object.

One by one, the 'workingmen' of the Holy City were found to be *talmidei chachamim*. "What am I and of what worth am I, when I compare myself to those great men who sit around the long table?" thought R' Yaakov to himself. He resolved to devote himself all the more to Torah and good deeds.

R' Yaakov's wealth allowed him and his wife Braina the opportunity to fulfill the verse, "Give of your bread to the hungry and bring the wretched poor into your house" (*Yeshayahu* 58:7). Their home was open day and night to those in need — to feed them and to support them generously. Even more than he was immersed in Torah study, he was involved in the work of charity.

In those days, people of means in Jerusalem could be counted on the fingers of one hand. And when R' Yaakov and his wife came from abroad with their great funds and their boundless energy in the pursuit of *chesed*, the poor and the suffering beat a path to their door. Even though they came in ever greater numbers, R' Yaakov and his wife never turned them away empty handed. To this one they gave money, to that one food; to one man a loan, to another a helping hand — each one according to his need. Yet they always felt that they had not done enough.

And so the years passed. R' Yaakov and his wife, through their good deeds and *chesed*, saw their dreams come true in their lifetime. But one day their happiness was threatened. R' Yaakov, while reviewing his accounts, discovered that he had given away a fifth of his resources as charity. He had reached the limit set by the Sages. The *halachah* was clear; he could give no more.

When he told his wife, Braina, of his decision, she began to cry and asked, bitterly, "And what will become of the poor people whom I secretly support; that large family for whom R'

Nissan Schuster makes shoes free of charge; the young mothers who have just given birth? You know that R' Leib, the milkman, fills their pitchers and runs away before they can pay him. And there are so many others. Far better that we should commit the sin of giving more than a fifth than that these families should starve and their children go barefoot. This certainly would be the sin to which the Sages referred when they said, 'Great is a sin committed with the proper intention!' "

But Braina's moving plea and learned remarks notwithstanding, R' Yaakov stood his ground. "Our Sages were like angels," he said. "They knew the measure and limit for every aspect of life. If they set a limit to charity, it was, certainly, not to hurt the poor. Rather, in their wisdom, they saw that even charity must have its limits. Look! The Rambam rules that one should always choose the middle path and avoid extremes. Extremism may be a subtle weapon of the evil nature (yetzer hara). When he sees that he cannot push a person off the path of good deeds, he persuades him to do a good deed to an excess. The man will more readily be snared. No! I will not depart from what the Sages have taught — a fifth and no more."

Braina, seeing that there was no way by which she could change her husband's mind, suggested that they should at least consult with a gadol beTorah before taking such a grave step. And off they went to Jerusalem's great rabbi, R' Shmuel Salant.

The old rav, having heard them out, sat facing them, tears streaming from his dim eyes. "Ribbono Shel Olam, Master of the Universe," he whispered, "who is like Your nation Yisrael? See what a man and his wife quarrel about? In my fifty years as dayan (judge), I have never encountered such a dispute!"

R' Shmuel took R' Yaakov's arm, patted it affectionately and said, "From all that I have heard about you, it is hard to imagine that you have ever sinned. Am I right?"

R' Yaakov shook his head in denial and humbly answered, "I'm no angel. Is it possible that a man of flesh and blood, whose evil inclination tempts him, day in day out, should not sin? Shlomo *HaMelech* said: 'There is not a man who does not sin.' And how, in particular, can I, a worthless fellow, who spent most of his years in the give-and-take of this world get up and say that I am clean from sin?"

"Then," said R' Shmuel, "the Sages don't forbid your giving more than a fifth of your possessions for charity. You have good reason to do so. Charity atones for sin. Does not Shlomo *HaMelech* say that *tzedakah* even saves one from death?

"I could not tell a sick man in need of a cure to spend only a fifth of what he has for the medicine which will save him. Anything and everything must be done to save him. Normally, charity has a limit. But your charity is an atonement, a cure. There is no limit. Go, R' Yaakov! Give charity and dispense as much *chesed* as you can; *Hashem* will surely lengthen your days."

Delighted by the ruling, R' Yaakov and his wife resumed their course of life and even increased the pace of their activity, until the day that Braina fell ill and took to her bed. When she felt her end was near, she summoned her husband and revealed the names of the families which she had secretly been supporting — families which would have starved without her help. She asked him to continue to take care of them and, after he had promised to do so, she tranquilly returned her soul to her Creator.

R' Yaakov continued to operate his *chesed* 'business.' Despite the loss of Braina and his advancing years, he did not curtail his schedule; he was busy from morning till night. He was particularly occupied on an *Erev Shabbos* or *Yom Tov*. And in the weeks before *Pesach*, he was a flurry of movement, rushing about from door to door, collecting from those who had and distributing to those who did not.

He insisted on either giving or taking. If someone would try to push him off with the excuse that, as of the moment, he was in somewhat tight circumstances, R' Yaakov would immediately reach into his pocket, pull out his list of takers and prepare to add the name of the hard-pressed soul. This little exercise worked wonders: "Please, R' Yaakov, not that," one would say. "I don't want my name on that list." There was only one way out — to give. And give he would.

⋙ The Missing Blessing

It was during such a hectic period of constant running about, that R' Yaakov returned home one evening weary and exhausted, as usual. The kerosene lamp flickered dimly, but R' Yaakov did not raise the wick. A higher flame meant a more rapid use of fuel. And he was willing to settle for the low light, provided he need not rise and refill the lantern. Tired as he was, that would require too great an effort. The table was spread with a clean white tablecloth. It was his longstanding custom to so honor the table, which symbolizes the Altar of Sacrifice. He made himself a small salad, adding salt and oil. He took out a round loaf of bread baked for him by the *tzaddekes*, Alte Feige the bakerwoman, and placed it on the table along with the salt and knife. He washed his hands and lifted them high, saying the customary: "*Se'u yedeichem kodesh...*" (lift up your hands in holiness — *Tehillim* 134:2). He pronounced the blessing, dried his hands and sat down to his usual small dinner after a day of almost total fasting, the bread in one hand, the knife in the other.

The old clock ticked monotonously; the flies and mosquitoes kept up an endless buzzing; the lantern sputtered and went out. R' Yaakov was fast asleep in his chair.

He awoke with a start. It was pitch black and, but for the chirp of the occasional cricket, all was quiet. He rubbed a hand across his eyes and threaded his way to the copper sink to wash his hands. He remembered that he had been in the middle of his meal. He turned to pick up the kettle and pour himself a hot drink but the fire had long since gone out and the water was cold. "But," thought R' Yaakov, "if I fell asleep while eating, I can no longer say the *Bircas Hamazon* (the after-the-meal blessing), for my food has long been digested." He knew that, because hunger gnawed at his stomach.

"Imagine, " he said aloud in his consternation, "that in my old age, I, R' Yaakov Galiner, should neglect to say *Bircas Hamazon*!" He smote his hands together, "What am I to do?" he lamented, "Master of the Universe, whence cometh my help? How am I to find rest for my soul when I have failed to fulfill a commandment of the Torah? See what loneliness and old age have wrought. If my Braina would be here, this would not have happened!"

And then, he thought, "It is already past midnight; R' Shmuel Salant will have risen by now to learn. I will go to him; perhaps, he can solve my problem."

R' Yaakov half stumbled, half ran to R' Shmuel's house in the Churva of R' Yehudah HeChasid. To his relief, there was a light in the window. With fear and reverence, he tapped on the door; it opened immediately.

R' Yaakov wrung his hands in despair. "Rabbi," he said, "I'm in trouble. Among my many sins, I fell asleep at the table in the middle of dinner and awoke after the food had been digested. I have lost my chance to say *Bircas Hamazon*."

"Do you know when you fell asleep and when you awoke? How can you be certain that you slept so long?" asked R' Shmuel.

"Is there any doubt? I'm hungry. What could be better proof than that?"

"That is not proof positive. But soon the morning star will rise. I suggest that you go to the Istanbuli synagogue in the R' Yochanan ben Zakkai building where our Sephardi brothers pray before they go to work. Invite one of the poor men to join you for breakfast. After the meal, he can have you in mind when he says *Bircas Hamazon* and you will thus fulfill your obligation, according to every opinion."

R' Yaakov felt as though a heavy weight had fallen away. He ran like a youth to the synagogue and found several *minyanim* of shopkeepers and laborers. He waited patiently for the completion of prayers and then approached a man who, from his shabby dress, appeared to be poor and begged him in his broken Hebrew (he generally spoke only Yiddish), "Please come for breakfast and say *Bircas Hamazon* for me. Have mercy on an old man. Come with me. It will be worth your while."

But the poor man was rushing off and he could not, for the life of him, make out what the old man wanted. Was he making a *simchah*? This early in the morning? He wanted to 'go out' (*latzeis*) in *Bircas Hamazon*? Surely he must know that one must say *Bircas Hamazon* where one eats; one may not leave. He must be confused in his old age. (R' Yaakov had meant that he wished to silently share in the blessings, but he could not make himself understood.) The poor workingman eluded him and escaped.

R' Yaakov pleaded again and again with each member of the *minyan*, without success. Each one went off to work. The synagogue had emptied and a desperate R' Yaakov ran out and clutched at the sleeve of an old Jew. "Thief!" he cried, "Have you no mercy on a Jew who has missed *Bircas Hamazon?* Have mercy on me!"

The old man looked on in perplexed pity and he, too, tried to leave, but R' Yaakov held on fast. The old man dragged the clinging R' Yaakov all the way to where Masuda the washerwoman did the clothes. She had spent many years helping Braina. Although herself a Sephardic Jew, she was fluent in Yiddish, from her many years among Ashkenazim. R' Yaakov explained the problem to her and she, in turn, made the matter clear to the old man.

Once he understood, the old Sephardi agreed to join R' Yaakov for breakfast, but first demanded the money. R' Yaakov had finally found a Jew who would free him from his plight.

Off they went, the old man, R' Yaakov, and Masuda in tow, should he once more need the services of a translator. A crowd of the curious had gathered about them. They reached R' Yaakov's home and R' Yaakov invited the old Sephardi and the washerwoman-translator in. He put down a setting for his guest, but could not find his loaf of bread.

"There it is under the table," cried Masuda, "fresh and whole; it's not been touched!"

Now it was all clear. R' Yaakov had fallen asleep and the loaf had dropped from his hands before he had said the blessing over it. He had not eaten even a morsel of food the night before.

Thus, R' Yaakov's problem turned out to be imaginary, and a poor Jew gained a little money and a good breakfast to boot.

Hashem saves the righteous from mishap. Happy is the people whose lot is such!

The Miracle of Kollel Minsk

Many new neighborhoods were established in Jerusalem outside the Old City walls in the very difficult years before and after World War I. One of these was Batei Minsk.

The residents of Jerusalem lived in various *kollelim*. Each *kollel* was a separate entity supported by the community of origin of the original settlers. Since local money was very scarce at the time, the *kollel* received a monthly allowance of support from the mother-community in the Diaspora. For was it not a *mitzvah* and an honor to help those who had gone up to *Eretz Yisrael* to pray on its holy soil and live a life of devotion there? Some of the larger and wealthier communities sent funds for building housing for the members of the *kollelim* which bore their name. Thus, Batei Varsha (Warsaw), Batei Ungarin (Hungary) and Batei Broyde came into existence.

Batei Minsk is a tiny, poor neighborhood, unknown to most, though it is but a short distance from the busy heart of the city. It looks more like a Lithuanian *shtetl* than part of a dynamic urban center. Behind its founding lies a miracle.

✄§ The Master Builder

One of the great builders of the time was R' Naftali Tzvi Porush. During his lifetime, he established no fewer than twelve new neighborhoods. He was one of the *Nekiyei Ha Da'as* (Clean of Thought), *tzaddikim* who were unique to Jerusalem.

His grandfather, R' Naftali Hirsh, had set out for *Eretz Yisrael* many years earlier, boarding an old rickety vessel in the Russian harbor of Odessa. He was tossed and turned on the wild seas until he reached Constantinople in Turkey. As if by a miracle, he arrived in *Eretz Yisrael* three months later. R' Naftali Hirsh understood what the sages meant when they said that the Holy Land is won through pain and suffering.

He made his home in the center of the Old City and walked to the *Kosel* every night. There he mourned for the *Beis HaMikdash* and cried the full tears of a little child.

And, when many years later, his grandson R' Naftali would pray, he, too, would cry copious tears. But when he said *U'vnei Yerushalayim*, the prayer for the rebuilding of Jerusalem, those tears would fall in a veritable stream. On *Tishah B'av*, he would walk barefoot from his home in Mishkenot to the *shul* in Batei Broyde, hat pulled low down over his eyes, lost in tragic thoughts. He would wander in his mind's eye through another world, in another time; he saw the *Beis HaMikdash* going up in flames and envisioned all the terrible scenes of *Megillas Eichah* and the *kinos*. R' Naftali would ponder the words of the Talmud's indictment: If the *Beis HaMikdash* is not rebuilt in a man's lifetime, it is as if it were destroyed in his lifetime. And that led him to become a great builder in Jerusalem.

After the death of his father, R' Shlomo Zalman Porush, R' Naftali was appointed head of Kollel Minsk. The winters grew colder; even bread was scarce. The future was generally uncertain. But it was certain that the Arab landlords would become greedier and greedier and raise the rents higher and higher, while the poor would become poorer.

R' Naftali had a burning desire to build, to build for the cold and the poor. He wanted to build homes for the rabbis who made Jerusalem a holy city. He persuaded the brothers, R' Baruch and R' Berel Zlodovitz, the "Rothschilds" of White Russia, to support the project. But even their generous contributions were not sufficient. All the donations amounted to only a fraction of what was needed to sustain the community. Besides, the Turkish overlords viewed with suspicion any attempt by the Jews to improve their situation.

Strange as it may seem, the very hopelessness of the Jews in Jerusalem discouraged those living abroad from being generous. R' Naftali's many appeals fell on deaf ears, until . . .

On the evening of the fourteenth of *Nisan* 5647 (1887), R' Naftali, after a long day spent in aiding the poor before *Pesach*, came home exhausted. Turning to his wife Yocheved, he asked if all was in readiness for *bedikas chametz,* the search for leaven; if the ten bits of bread had been placed throughout the house. She reassured him that everything had been prepared. R' Naftali removed his overcoat, lit the wax taper and began the search. When the ten hidden pieces had been found, he was filled with a sense of satisfaction and joy; he had performed the *mitzvah* as the Rabbis had directed! His fatigue was forgotten.

The family ate their last *chametz* meal by the flickering light of one small candle. They crowded around a huge basin that held the *chametz* which as yet remained, necks stretched over the rim to prevent the dropping of even a single crumb onto the scrubbed floor.

After they had eaten the last morsel, R' Naftali stepped out into the courtyard to brush off his clothing three times, as was his custom. He was about to reenter his home, when R' Lebel Cohen, the *kollel gabai* appeared, suddenly, clutching a telegram. It was from Russia, from R' Berel Zlodovitz, the president of the *kollel*. It was short but clear: Please pray for the young Eliyahu Baruch ben Mushka who has wandered from the proper path.

◆§ The Prayer

R' Naftali realized that the matter was urgent. He and R' Lebel gathered a *minyan*. Midnight came and ten of the finest and most pious Jews of *Yerushalayim* assembled at the *Kosel*, the Western Wall. For hours they stood and prayed for Eliyahu ben Mushka.

R' Naftali recorded the event in his diary:

> "We were all very moved, as we prayed fervently, clinging to the holy stones of the *Kosel*. We pleaded with the Almighty to sanctify the holy name of *Yerushalayim* and to accept the prayers of its sons. Nothing could stop us as we continued to recite *Tikkun Chatzos*, the prayer mourning the loss of our *Beis HaMikdash*. We returned

home, hopeful that our prayers had soared to Heaven and were accepted by the Master of the universe.''

◄§ The Miracle

At that very moment, when the righteous of *Yerushalayim* were clinging to the stones of the *Kosel*, another, very different drama was taking place far away in Minsk.

Eliyahu Baruch was the only son of the great benefactor R' Hershel Zlodovitz, brother to R' Berel, president of the *kollel* of Minsk in Jerusalem. Tragedy struck. Pneumonia carried off R' Hershel in the prime of life and, with his death, he left behind a great fortune to his only son.

Great wealth, however, as it often does, cast an unsettling influence on the lad. Eliyahu Baruch began to associate with young people for whom pleasure was the important goal in life. He immersed himself in a life of merrymaking and foolishness. He left his mother's home and, with his new-found friends, rented an apartment in the middle of town.

And as he left his mother's home, he wandered away from the path of his traditions. His new acquaintances were rogues who did not care for Eliyahu Baruch. They were just out to take advantage of his wealth and immaturity. They prodded and pushed him from one adventure to the next. And in the process, he fell lower and lower. Soon he began to eat non-kosher food, to desecrate the *Shabbos* and to deny G-d's existence. His pained family looked on with shame and horror.

Every year the Zlodovitz family conducted a *seder* in grand style at the villa of R' Berel Zlodovitz. As *Pesach* approached, Mushka, the mother of Eliyahu Baruch, sent for her son and tearfully pleaded with him to join the family at Uncle Berel's.

Not only did the boy flatly refuse, but he was offensive. "A family *seder*? Do I have nothing better to do with my time? Why, I have made my own plans with my friends and we're going to have a real party. Do you expect me to pass that up and attend a *seder*?"

Mushka screamed and fainted. Only after great effort did her maid manage to restore her. Slowly, the poor mother made her way to her brother-in-law's home to seek his advice.

"What shall I do, Berel?" she said. "He's my son, my only son. I must save him."

Berel Zlodovitz sank deep in thought. True, he was a grandee of Minsk, one of the most powerful men of Russia, but at that moment he felt powerless. For Mushka, the silence was overwhelming.

Finally, he spoke, "We have never been so tested. Eliyahu Baruch is caught in a trap beyond our understanding; only a miracle can save him. Mushka, we must pray as we have never prayed before in all of our lives."

He fell silent once more, and then, all of a sudden, his face lit up; his eyes shone; he had made a great discovery. "What about the *kollel* in *Yerushalayim*?" he said. "We have been fortunate enough to support the holy men of *Yerushalayim*. They can reach out to Heaven. Certainly, their prayers will not go unheeded! I will speak to my brother, Baruch, the *kollel's* president. He will send them a telegram. They will pray for your son, Mushka and their prayers shall be answered."

And so, in the dead of the night before *Pesach*, the men prayed in *Yerushalayim* and, as they prayed, a frightened youth approached a small house in Minsk. His knees trembled as he jumped over a familiar gate. He breathed deeply and tapped twice on the shuttered window, but there was no response. He tapped again, but to no avail.

Within the house sat two frightened women; Mushka, the widow of R' Hershel, and her elderly mother. Both stared at the window. Who was outside at this hour? They put out their lantern, and listened. They were shocked when they heard the voice of Eliyahu Baruch call out and beg, "Mother! Grandmother! Please! It is I. It's Eliyahu Baruch. Open up, I must speak to you!"

They could not believe their ears. The tapping grew louder and more persistent; the voice, the familiar voice, sounded desperate. Finally, they mustered up the courage and, with shaking hands, opened the door.

Before them stood the young boy shivering like a leaf in a winter wind. He was choking in his tears, as he began to pour out his heart.

"Forgive me, Mother, for all the grief that I have caused you. Please! Take me back into the warmth and loving kindness of our family. Ask Uncle Berel to forgive me and to allow me to sit at the *seder* table together with the rest of the family."

After regaining his composure, Eliyahu Baruch told his mother and grandmother what had happened.

"I climbed into bed exhausted, but for some reason I could not fall asleep. Suddenly, I saw before my eyes the tall figure of my late father. He spoke to me. I could not believe it. He kept repeating, 'Eliyahu Baruch go home. Return from your evil and crooked ways.'

"I was terrified. I pulled the cover over my head and tried to be calm. I shut my eyes, but I could not escape the familiar voice. It sounded like a pleading cry, 'Eli, my Eli Baruch, go home to Mama.'

"I removed my blanket and lit a candle. There was my dear father standing before me and begging. His stare pierced my heart. And that is why I am here."

Before morning, R' Berel learned that Eliyahu Baruch had returned to the family fold. Word traveled so rapidly that when the Jews of Minsk stood by their fires burning their *chametz*, all knew of the great miracle that had just taken place. They all spoke of the boy who had gone astray and had now returned to his family.

◆§ The Kollel

On the second day of *Pesach* when the elders of Minsk gathered around the table of R' Berel Zlodovitz for their customary feast, all spoke excitedly of the great miracle that had happened to young Eliyahu Baruch. R' Naftali Maskil LuEitan, the treasurer of the *kollel*, arose and spoke of the telegram and the role played by the men of *Yerushalayim*.

"See, how precious are these pious men of *Yerushalayim*," he said. "Without their prayers there could have been no miracle. Now, I believe, the time has come to settle an old debt with the members of our *kollel*.

"These men and their families have been asking us for years to help them build homes for their poor. And we have never even answered their requests, let alone helped them."

The hushed room was quickly thrown into a hubbub as people pledged their support. The Zlodovitz family alone, Eliyahu Baruch included, donated four thousand ruble.

With this money, land was purchased between the Knesset Yisrael neighborhood and today's Bezalel Street. On this property the Kollel Minsk was built. It originally bore the name, "Shechunat Beit Levi" in honor of the Zlodovitz family who were *Leviim*.

The *gabbaim* made sure that every square inch of land was

put to use. They sowed wheat for *shmurah matzah* on the field in front of the *kollel* buildings. R' Mottel Milner set up his mill on the western corner of the property (unfortunately, it was destroyed in a fire some twenty years ago); on the northern side R' Chaim Halperin erected his bakery — the well-known Cohen-Halperin Matzah Bakery which serves the people of *Yerushalayim* to this very day.

Mitzvah Follows Mitzvah

His name was R' Shlomo Zalman Loewe, but he was known as R' Zalman-R' Nachum's — that is, R' Zalman the son of R' Nachum. And so he is called to this day, nearly eighty years after his death.

His father was the Torah giant and *tzaddik* R' Nachum Shadiker. It was said, in his time, that Eliyahu *HaNavi* had appeared to R' Nachum and that he was one of the *lamed vavniks*, the thirty-six *tzaddikim* of each age in whose merit the world continues to exist.

One night R' Nachum dreamt that he saw an angel-like figure who spoke to him and said, "How long will you be like one in a stupor, not knowing what to do? Get up and go to Jerusalem, and *Hashem* will be with you in whatever you do and wherever you go." R' Nachum saw this as a sign from Heaven and decided, then and there, to go up to *Eretz Yisrael*.

Several days before he set out on the long journey, his brothers, R' Asher Lemmel, *av beis din* of Galin, and R' Yaakov Leib came to say farewell. When he told them of his dream, they said that the angel-like being had appeared to each of them, also, and spoken the identical words. They both joined him and all three went up to *Eretz Yisrael* together.

They left at the end of *Nisan* 5603 (1883) and arrived in *Tammuz* of the following year — fourteen months of trials and tribulation. Jerusalem received them with honor and they were known as the "three holy brothers."

R' Zalman-R' Nachum's was eight years old when he arrived in *Eretz Yisrael* where he was to spend a lifetime helping and teaching others, always free of charge. For just as *Hashem* taught Moshe Rabbenu without pay, so, *Chazal* say, we are to teach others without pay. And just as *Hashem* is merciful, so are we to imitate His ways and show compassion to all. This was R' Zalman's creed.

He was first and foremost whenever there was a need; he was an address to whom all turned.

In the week of *parashas Toldos*, in the year 5634 (1873), the then-small Jewish community of Jerusalem was in a ferment. A wealthy Arab *effendi* had evicted a Jewish tenant from a flat on Chevron Street. The Jew had refused to accept an arbitrary increase of rent and the Arab had promptly had his belongings thrown out onto the public thoroughfare.

On Friday afternoon, when R' Zalman came for his customary immersion before *Shabbos*, in the *mikveh* below the Tiferes Yisrael synagogue of R' Nissan Beck, he found a group of angry Jews. Tempers were high. Everyone asked the same question, "How long will we be trampled on by these

Ishmaelites, who oppress us without pity?" And everyone turned to R' Zalman with the identical plea, "R' Zalman, save us from these Ishmaelites. If you can't, then no one can!"

R' Zalman entered the steaming, hot *mikveh*, emerged, dried himself, dressed and wrapped a towel around his neck as a protection against drafts. He made his way to the passage near the entrance, lined with long benches. It served as a cooling area for those who had just come from the *mikveh* and the steambath, and it did double duty as an informal council chamber for the community. The men sitting there had just purified themselves in honor of the approaching *Shabbos*. Normally, they would be resting, breathing easily, beads of perspiration slowly drying on their foreheads, in the relatively cool air — at peace with the world and themselves. But not this day. A Jew had been thrown out of his home. Burning words of anger swirled about. R' Zalman entered the passageway; all eyes turned towards him and there was dead silence.

R' Zalman wiped his brow and announced in a strong voice, intense with feeling, "I shall not rest until I have broken the power of the oppressors. Tomorrow evening, one hour after the departure of the *Shabbos*, let us all meet at the Menachem Zion synagogue in the Churva of R' Yehudah HeChasid. We will draw up plans to break out of these straits and *Hashem* who loves Zion and rebuilds Jerusalem will come to our aid. If ten *minyanim*, one hundred Jews, are willing to take part in the task of building Jerusalem, I will know that you are sincere and that the spirit of *Hashem* moves within you. We will, then, surely rebuild the ruins of Jerusalem together!"

R' Zalman did not go straight home. He took a detour to the fine house of R' Ben Zion Leon. R' Ben Zion had sold all his property in the Diaspora and came to live in Jerusalem to help it grow. When R' Zalman was shown in at this unusual hour before *Shabbos*, R' Ben Zion had been reviewing the weekly *parashah* — *sh'nayim mikra v'echad targum* (twice in the Hebrew and once in the Aramaic version of Onkelos). He closed the *chumash* and welcomed his unexpected guest warmly. R' Zalman revealed his plan and R' Ben Zion enthusiastically agreed to help.

On *Motzaei Shabbos,* exactly ten *minyanim* assembled. R' Zalman addressed the gathering as follows:

"Blessed are all of you who come in the name of *Hashem*, for the sake of our people and the city of our G-d. We all wish to restore the greatness of Jerusalem and to rebuild its ruins. Jerusalem, too, yearns to gather in her beloved children. And what prevents this? Fear! If one hundred pioneers will come forward and remove this fear from their hearts, they will go their way in peace and the whole of the people will follow after them. The first one hundred shall bring merit to us all. Each one will open a single gate and together, all in all, *meah shearim* — a hundred gates!"

Then and there, money was collected to buy a plot of land beyond the walls of the city. The event was recorded in writing and the document was duly signed by all present. The date was alluded to in the following manner:

> On *Motzaei Shabbos, parashas* 'and Yitzchak planted in that land and he found in that year that he harvested a hundred-fold (*meah shearim*) and *Hashem* blessed him' (*Bereishis* 26:12).

When the others had left, R' Ben Zion approached R' Zalman and said confidently, "Tomorrow, with G-d's help, let us go and examine a site for the neighborhood. Whatever we need as a down payment can come out of my own pocket."

And on the following morning, the two men went out to

survey an area called Karm Kadkod, some ten minutes from the Damascus gate. That very same day they bought a plot of some twenty-five thousand square cubits (roughly, six thousand square feet) for the price of twenty-nine thousand, six hundred and eight Turkish *grushim* for the new neighborhood of Meah Shearim.

By *Chanukah* 5635 (1874), the first ten houses were already completed and the first residents of the new neighborhood, who had formerly lived in the Old City, moved in, to the sounds of an enthusiastic celebration. R' Zalman, himself, danced ahead of the wagons which brought them and their belongings. But it would not be until 5643 (1883) that all one hundred and one homes would be standing.

The new neighborhood lay in unfenced fields, and the nervous newcomers felt that they were easy prey for bands of thieves. R' Zalman stayed with them that first night, and they drew courage from his strength.

R' Zalman spent a watchful night in his brother R' Avraham's home. Had he tried, he would have been unable to sleep. He was thrilled by the realization of his dream. The first homes stood where there had been but barren rock, proclaiming to the world the redemption of the desolation of Zion and the ruins of Jerusalem.

Morning came. They prayed in a temporary *shul*. R' Zalman led them in *Mizmor shir chanukas haBayis* (A hymn, the song of dedication of The House — *Tehillim* 30, which David wrote for the dedication of the Temple) to a tune which he had composed for the occasion. Everyone repeated each verse after him.

They sang *Hallel* that *Chanukah* morning, as if it had been written for just that day and most especially so, when they reached '*min hametzar karasi k-ah, anani vamerchav k-ah*' (from a straightened place I called forth to *Hashem* and *Hashem* answered me by placing me in broad regions). The *'zeh hayom asah Hashem, nagilah v'nismechah vo'* (this is the day that *Hashem* made; we will be happy and rejoice upon it) swelled forth in song. They gave voice to a thunderous *'ana Hashem hoshiah na; ana Hashem hatzlichah na'* (*Hashem*, save us, we beg you; let us be successful, *Hashem*, we beg you).

But as they were concluding their *Hallel*, there burst forth a sound of a different sort — the shriek of a child in agony. Little Nachum Yitzchak, the son of R' Zalman's brother R' Avraham, had been playing among the flowers which grew wild around the houses and had been bitten by a poisonous scorpion. His screams drew them all. His poor mother wrung her hands and wept helplessly. Only R' Zalman remained calm.

He quickly seized the bitten finger of the youngster and, deliberately thrusting it in his mouth, sucked at the wound to draw forth the poison, which he spat out. He continued his treatment, until the swelling subsided. The crowd gazed with wonder and admiration, as if they had witnessed a miracle.

R' Zalman turned to them and said, "Friends, the attack on the lad by the scorpion was the work of the wicked Edom, who suffers when he sees us redeeming the land. The powers of evil have many agents, who take on many disguises, to stop Israel from resettling and rebuilding the Holy City, for they feed on ruin and desolation. Nothing shall frighten us and no obstacle shall stop us from restoring Zion to its past glory. We will rebuild the ruins and drive out desolation.

"Friends, front-line troops of *Mashiach*, have no fear. The tradition has come down to me from my father, of blessed memory, that when *Chazal* said that neither snake nor scorpion ever harmed anyone in Jerusalem it was not only true for the Temple area, but for all of Jerusalem, and it was not only true when the Temple stood, but it was to be true for all time. That is why they began by saying that ten miracles took place in the Temple but include this one which applies to Jerusalem. I am, therefore, certain that we will live to see *Chazal's* words fulfilled in a renewed Jerusalem where enemies will not harm us — not Edom, not Ishmael, not snakes, not scorpions. And this boy, Nachum Yitzchak ben Chayah Gittel, will surely be healed by Him Who chose Jerusalem and Who heals all men."

◁§ The Drought

That year was a year of drought. *Kislev* was almost over and the rains had not yet begun to fall. The large cistern in the middle of the new neighborhood was empty; the well had run dry. And who could buy water at the sky-high prices demanded by the Arabs? R' Zalman was deeply concerned about the fate of the infant settlement he had fathered.

R' Zalman had another problem which concerned not the community as a whole, but a single individual. Nevertheless, it was a serious problem which plagued him. He had a gifted student who stood head and shoulders above his peers. His knowledge was broad in scope, his understanding profound; he was exceptional, yet humble. He was all that a *talmid chacham* should be. Shmuel Chaim lacked but one thing — money; his family was poor.

Shmuel Chaim had become engaged to a fine girl of a good family with all the right qualities one expects in the wife of a *talmid chacham*, but her family, too, was poor.

Several months had elapsed since their engagement, but no date had as yet been set for the marriage. Funds were not available and Shmuel Chaim lost his customary glow of contentment. R' Zalman was determined to find the means for the marriage somewhere, somehow!

R' Zalman-R' Nachum's paid his nephew, R' Zalman-R'Yaakov Leib's, a call and made a proposition. "Let us have our *mitzvah* of *yishuv Eretz Yisrael* (settling the land) pull along another *mitzvah* in its wake," he said. "To date we have only erected ten houses in Meah Shearim. It will be some time before the rest are put up. If we plant wheat on the open field we will have a harvest which the *shmurah matzah* bakeries will snatch from our hands. The proceeds will allow us to involve ourselves in yet another, a third *mitzvah*; we will be able to provide Shmuel Chaim with a fine wedding and bring him and his deserving *kallah* to the *chupah*."

The next morning the two R' Zalman's, uncle and nephew, left the Damascus Gate for Meah Shearim, hoes over their shoulders. They spent several days preparing the soil — removing rocks, hoeing, raking; the field was ready to be planted.

R' Zalman then visited R' Yedidiah, Shmuel Chaim's father. He touched upon the topic of Shmuel Chaim's unhappy state and its cause. R' Yedidiah heaved a sigh and said, " But what can I do? I have always prayed that *Hashem* supply my wants and not man. For food which comes from G-d, though it be as bitter as a leaf from an olive tree, is sweeter in my eyes than honey which would be offered by flesh and blood. I will not accept charity nor even undertake a loan. For I do not know how I can repay it."

R' Zalman did not suggest charity or a loan. He offered to make R' Yedidiah a partner in the wheat-growing project. R' Yedidiah would have to supply the capital for the purchase of seed.

R' Yedidiah agreed wholeheartedly. He drew out a gold

bracelet, which had been his mother's, from a wooden chest and handed it to R' Zalman. "Here's your capital," he said. "Sell this and buy your grain seed."

The following day, R' Zalman went to the office of the Shaarei Chesed G'mach (free-loan society) where R' Shlomo Zalman Porush sat, supervising the granting of loans. The bracelet served as collateral. With the money he obtained, he bought a bag of seed, and the two R' Zalmans plowed the field and sowed the seed.

But the rains had not yet come and it was the middle of *Teves.*

The uncle and nephew left the field and made their way back to the Old City, to the *Kosel Hamaaravi* and thus, the two Zalmans prayed:

"Our Father, merciful and forgiving Father, our pains and our labor have been for the sake of a *mitzvah.* Show pity and compassion. Let our efforts not have been in vain. We have done ours; now You do Yours and send Your blessing on Your holy land and city. Let Your face shine upon us and we will be saved."

On their way home R' Zalman-R' Nachum's said to his nephew, R' Zalman-R' Yaakov Leib's, "My father would often say that two *mitzvos* such as providing for a bride and participating in the *mitzvah* of *matzah* make their mark upon Heaven. I am sure that they will bring an answer to our prayer."

Towards evening, the sky became overcast. Soon a pelting rain of blessing fell. For an entire day it continued, soaking the parched earth in its abundance. And once the gates of Heaven had opened, they remained open. The cisterns were filled to overflowing, the sources of the springs were replenished. Jerusalem and *Eretz Yisrael* drank deeply and quenched their thirst. A rainy season of such proportions was rare.

Nisan arrived and Meah Shearim boasted a field of wheat.

R' Zalman took R' Yedidiah to the field. "We are told," he said, "that Elazar ben Birta went out to make arrangements for his daughter's wedding. On the way he met the officials in charge of charity, who were collecting for a needy bride. He gave them the entire sum which he had with him except for a single *zuz*. With that one coin he bought a measure of wheat which he put in the warehouse. It increased and increased until it filled the warehouse. So, too, the Holy One, Blessed is He, has done us a *chesed*, a kindness, and filled the entire field with wheat for *matzah*. And it is all yours, for it is from the seed which we bought with your money."

R' Yedidiah's eyes filled with tears of joy and that very day he took out a loan; the wheat served as his security. He immediately arranged for a wedding.

A week before *Pesach*, Shmuel Chaim and the *kallah* Ita Perel went under the *chupah* and all of Jerusalem rejoiced and was happy.

And a Great Shofar
Will Be Blown

Go ask, even the old-timers of Jerusalem, if they remember a Jewish neighborhood called Ezrat Nidchim. It stood at the foot of the Mount of Olives, east of the valley of Yehoshafat and the Kidron brook, near the Arab village of Silwan. They will tell you that they never heard of any such neighborhood. But add another detail, that it was also known as Kfar Hashiloach. Then, heads will nod knowledgeably. They will recall that, indeed, there was a Yemenite enclave on the slopes of the Mount of Olives, not far from the grave of the prophet Zechariah.

When they entered upon the year 5642 (1882), our

brothers in Yemen were certain that the Redemption was close at hand. For did not Shlomo *HaMelech* say, "I will go up in the date tree" — בתמר (*Shir HaShirim* 7:9), and are those letters not an allusion to the year תרמ״ב (5642)? Many did not hesitate; they sold their possessions and began the trek across the Arabian desert. To the Holy Land! To the Holy Land! They would see the herald of the *Mashiach* when he appeared on the heights of *Har Hazeisim*, the Mount of Olives. They would be among the first to greet the *Mashiach* himself!

The journey was one hardship after another. Robbers waylaid them and took whatever they had and they often reached *Eretz Yisrael* with nothing but the clothes on their back. They tried to find lodgings in the Old City, but the Arab landlords demanded rents beyond their reach. An issue of the magazine, *HaAsif*, from the year 5646 (1886), describes their plight:

> Our brothers from Yemen lack the funds to rent houses; they sleep in the streets and find clefts in the rocks and caves in the hills surrounding Jerusalem and live there. Day and night they wander about the city asking for food for their little ones and they find refuge in holes where their bones shake from cold and fear.

The Yemenites were to suffer for more than three years, until the Ezrat Nidchim Society came to their aid. It gathered just enough money to build ten houses on a field owned by a man named Boaz Bavli and these were given to the Yemenites. A year later, a number of philanthropists could no longer stand by and witness the suffering of the immigrants. Baron Hirsch of Argentina, Yosef Bey Navon, Yosef Kokya and Rabbi Dr. Splandy, among others, contributed funds for building. By the year 5658 (1898), sixty-five structures stood in Kfar Hashiloach. One hundred and seventy-five families, the majority from Yemen, found shelter there. Good relations prevailed between the Jews and their Arab neighbors until the outbreak of the riots in 5696 (1936). Because of the hatred fomented by the Mufti of Jerusalem, the Jews abandoned their homes and Arabs from Silwan and other nearby villages moved in.

ᴇᴈ To Greet Mashiach

One of the first to settle in Kfar Hashiloach was Mori Saadiah who went up to Israel from San'a in Yemen, with his wife and three sons. He had neither means nor profession, but managed to eke out a bare living by taking on whatever work he could find. But he did not complain. On the contrary, he rejoiced in his lot and his lips were constantly praising and thanking Him Who dwelt in the Heavens. For did he not live near the site of the *Beis HaMikdash*; could he not pour out his heart at the Western Wall from which the *Shechinah* (the Divine Presence) had never moved? He would stand for long hours at the window of his home and look out, tense and expectant, waiting for the *Mashiach* who might come at any moment, fulfilling the prophecy of Zechariah the prophet: "And his feet will stand on that day on the Mount of Olives which faces Jerusalem on the east" (*Zechariah* 14:4).

"My house is small and narrow," Mori Saadiah would tell his friends, "but it rests by the Mount of Olives and if *Hashem* grants it, I will be among the first ten to greet the *Mashiach.*"

At the end of his first year in *Eretz Yisrael,* Mori Saadiah and his wife were blessed with another child, a fine-looking son. There was no doubt as to what name the child should bear. The boy was the fourth in the family, the first to be born in the shadow of Jerusalem, since the return from the Exile in Yemen, where his fathers and fathers' fathers before them had lived from the time of the destruction of the First Temple. He had been born only a few short steps away from the grave of the prophet Zechariah. What greater pleasure of the spirit could there be for the soul of the prophet, who saw the return of Israel to its land in his vision of the Redemption, than to call the child by his name. And so they did.

Little Zechariah was alert, with a weave of charm playing across his shining face. And when Mori Saadiah played with the infant, he would say reverently, "How lovely are the young of Jerusalem. None can compare to them for beauty. The *Shechinah* hovers over them from the moment they come into the world. I am certain that a spark of the soul of the prophet Zechariah is found in the soul of this son of mine. Would that I be allowed to bring him up to embark on a life of Torah, to lead him to the *chupah* and have him accomplish good deeds. Would that I be found worthy to take him to greet our king, the *Mashiach*, when he will descend the Mount of Olives and pass by our home, speedily in our days."

~§ In the Shade of the Fig Tree

In the courtyard of Mori Saadiah's house grew a magnificent fig tree that spread its shade across the entire area. When, with the lengthening shadows of the late afternoon, Mori Saadiah would return home from a hard day of whatever labor he had found, he would sit relaxed on a stool at the foot of the tree, lean his weary back against its comforting trunk and sing songs, songs saturated with longing for Jerusalem and Zion. Joy and longing mingled; pain and pleasure looked out from his jet-black eyes. And three delightful, lively children, curled *peyos* (sidelocks) down to their shoulders, jostled and nestled around him. A light evening breeze would whisper through the branches, bringing cooling relief. At such moments, Mori Saadiah might very well give voice to his uppermost thoughts, "Blessed and praised is His great Name that I am granted what my father and my father's father were denied. I draw breath in the clear, pure air of the Holy City and the Sanctuary; I find shelter under this fig tree which gives forth a smell of the Garden of Eden. Praised is the great Name of the Creator, blessed forever and all time." And he would fix his gaze on the path that twists and turns its way down from the crest of the mountain and murmur, "Here, down this path, the *Mashiach* will come, after the great blast of the *shofar* has been sounded, the *tekiah gedolah*, which will proclaim to Israel and the world that the Redemption has arrived."

Mori Saadiah was content, and more than content; he was happy with his lot. In what he had of free time, he would study and perform *mitzvos*, with fear and trembling. Of all, the *mitzvah* most beloved to him was *succah*. He would try to fulfill the obligation to sit in the *succah* for seven days, as perfectly as possible, following each detail outlined in the works of the Yemenite kabbalist, R' Shalom Shar'abi. On *Rosh Chodesh Elul*, he would begin to gather materials for the construction of the *succah*. He would hang the interior with silk sheets, embroidered works and precious carpets, heirlooms from the generations past, which he had managed to bring from Yemen. From *Motzaei Yom Kippur* until the eve of the Festival, Mori Saadiah and his children prepared decorations of flowers and shiny colored paper to adorn the walls of the *succah*.

Mori Saadiah was content and happy with his lot throughout the year, but his cup of joy was filled to overflowing on

Succos. He would fulfill the *mitzvah* of "you shall rejoice in your Festival, you and your household" with every limb and organ. And from the first day of *Succos* to the last, he never ceased murmuring, "Oh that I might soon rejoice in the *simchas beis hasho'evah* in the Temple, may it speedily be rebuilt, and that I, with my own eyes, might see the crowds come down with tambourines and bells to the Kidron valley to draw water from the spring of the Shiloach."

It was the custom in Kfar Hashiloach that on one of the nights of *Chol HaMoed*, the entire settlement — men, women and children, the young and the old — would gather in the *succah* of Mori Saadiah for a *simchas beis hasho'evah*. With deep-seated longing of the spirit, they would pour forth the songs of Redemption by the Yemenite poet R' Shalom Shazbi, bodies swaying back and forth to the rhythm of flute and drum. The sound echoed and reechoed, reaching even as far as the homes of the Jews within the walls. And then, it would ebb away and a hush would envelop the gathering. Mori Saadiah would mount a table, the great *shofar* he had brought with him from Yemen in hand, and send forth a '*tekiah, shevarim teruah, tekiah*.' The assembled would intone, "Just as we have heard the sound of this *shofar*, may we be found worthy to hear the sound of the *shofar* of the *Mashiach*, may he come soon, in our day," whereupon the music and the singing were renewed with greater force and vigor.

On *Hoshana Rabbah*, the day on which, traditionally, the Redemption is to take place, Mori Saadiah was all expectation. The moment arrived during the morning prayers when he was to pronounce the prayer which describes the Redemption and beat the *aravah* on the ground. His body would shake as he called out in a mighty voice, "*Kol mevaser, mevaser v'omer*!" (a voice brings news, brings news and proclaims) and beat the *aravah*. He would wield it until all its leaves had fallen.

Mori Saadiah had a birchwood staff which had been passed down from father to son, generation after generation. Family tradition had it that his ancestor had leaned on it when he led the family into exile after the destruction of the First Temple. And the tradition related that he who took the staff with him to Zion would run with it to greet the *Mashiach*. During the year, the staff was hidden away, but on *Hoshana Rabbah* it made its appearance. Mori Saadiah would sit in the *succah* the entire day, staff near at hand, taut as a violin string, expecting, at any moment, to hear the sound of the *shofar* and see the herald descend the mountain.

⋑§ Lost and Found

The fig tree in the courtyard did more than provide cool shade from the heat of the day; it also served to supplement Mori Saadiah's income. In the late summer, once the fruit began to ripen, he would fill a basket with juicy figs each day, set aside the *terumos* and *ma'asros* and climb the twisting path to the Old City. There, he would find a spot in a corner of the market which ran between HaYehudim Street and HaShalshelet Street. He usually had little difficulty selling his produce. The figs were practically snatched out of his hands. They were excellent and, besides, the women preferred to buy from the wiry Yemenite, with his *peyos* drifting down to his shoulders, rather than from the Arab women.

Zechariah, the son of his old age, would regularly accompany him. And it was Zechariah who weighed the figs for the customers with professional competence. When he had

given the requested amount, Zechariah would add a fig; his father had taught him that it was better to give a little more than to stumble into sin by giving short weight. When business was slow, Zechariah would play with the children of the Arab shopkeepers. They were fond of him, and showered him with sweets and little gifts, even inviting him into their homes. Zechariah was an especially close friend of Fouad, the only son of a grocer who lived in Kfar al-Azariah.

One day, when Mori Saadiah had sold the last of his figs, he packed his scales and prepared to return home. His little son was not in sight and, as he often did, he raised his voice and called out, "Zechariah! Zechariah! Come quickly, now! Time to go home." Zechariah had always heard and would dart out of an alley, or a store, and rush into his father's arms.

But this time there was no response. Mori Saadiah ran from alley to alley, from shop to shop, but little Zechariah could not be found. Several shopkeepers had seen the boy earlier with the other children, playing their usual pranks, but had paid them no attention. The Turkish gendarmes arrived and searched in vain. The sergeant in charge was unmoved. "We have a long list of lost children," he said. "Be patient and hope that he will return home, healthy and whole."

A broken Mori Saadiah made his way back to Kfar Hashiloach and broke the bitter news to his wife. At first she was thunderstruck and then a stream of tears burst forth; she pulled at her hair and gave vent to bitter cries. All efforts to calm her failed.

From that day forward, the joy of Mori Saadiah disappeared. He mourned his lost son day and night, when the world slept and in its waking hours. Thirty days passed and, still, his sorrow was as vividly painful as it had been that first day. And because of the intensity of that sorrow, he began to comfort himself. Beyond a doubt, his son was alive. Were he not, the memory would be a trifle dimmer, the pain would have subsided somewhat. For do not our Sages say that it has been decreed that the truly dead are forgotten from the heart (*Pesachim* 54b)? And so, Mori Saadiah would make it a practice to visit the nearby grave of the prophet Zechariah each day. There he would light a candle and murmur, "Just as this is lit and shines, so may the candle of my son Zechariah, who was named for the holy prophet, still shine." He opened his hand in charity, far beyond the measure of his purse; he prayed by the grave of Rachel *Imeinu*; he prostrated himself on the graves of *tzaddikim*; he consulted the wise rabbis and kabbalists among the Yemenites.

Days passed; many days. They stretched into weeks; weeks into months. As *Succos* approached, doubt tore at the heart of Mori Saadiah. Should he build his mammoth *succah* and be host for the *simchas beis hasho'evah*, as had been his practice, or, out of mourning for his son, would restraint be more proper? The elders of the community advised him not to depart from his custom. "On the contrary," they said, "notwithstanding your suffering, this year you must be more joyous, and by the merit of your joy, you and all of us will gain deliverance. And do not forget to blow your great *shofar* which may lead us to Redemption. Does not the prophet say, 'On that day a great *shofar* will be blown and those who are perishing shall come from the land of Ashur and the dispersed in the land of Egypt.' "

On the second night of *Chol HaMoed*, as they had done year after year, they gathered in Mori Saadiah's *succah* to celebrate the *simchas beis hasho'evah*. In the stillness of the night the sound of flute and drum carried from Kfar Hashiloach all the way to Kfar al-Azariah. Little Zechariah lay on a bed in the house of his friend Fouad. He was not asleep and, yet, not fully awake, in an almost trance-like state, barely aware of the far-off music. The music ceased and then — *tekiah, shevarim teruah, tekiah gedolah* — the call of the great *shofar* reached his ear; something stirred deep within a tender Jewish soul. Somewhere in his past he had heard such sounds. A pause, and then once more the trill of the flute, the beat of the drum. His heart pulsed to that beat and a yearning for something lost came over him. He sat up; he stood; he went where his feet carried him — drawn to the music. One slow step and then another. Then matching the beat and the lilt of the melody he skipped over the path to Kfar Shiloach.

From behind the wide trunk of the fig tree, the youngster peeked into the *succah*. There in the circle of the dance were his brothers; there was his beloved father. With a swift motion, he entered the *succah* and joined the dancers. Someone noticed him and burst out, "He's here! He's here! Zechariah! Zechariah!" His father drew near, stared and fainted.

Mori Saadiah came to. He and his wife hugged and kissed the boy. Yet, Zechariah was unable to explain his disappearance. He mumbled something about being a guest in the house of his friend Fouad, but nothing more. What had happened? Why had the Arabs not brought him home? These questions were left unanswered. They would conduct a thorough investigation immediately after *Succos*.

Meanwhile, their joy knew no bounds. Their happiness spilled over and embraced the entire community. And it was said of that night of rejoicing, just as our Sages have said of the *simchas beis hasho'evah* in the *Beis HaMikdash* itself, "Whoever did not witness that expression of joy never witnessed joy in his life."

The Two Napoleons

In the last century, in the village of Volkovysk, Lithuania, lived a righteous learned Jew known as R' Zelig the Parush. Every *Motzaei Shabbos* he would leave his family and seclude himself (*poresh* — go into retreat) for the entire week in the women's section of the Craftsmen's Society Synagogue. There he would study and pray.

Heaven did not mete out a rich lot in worldly goods to R' Zelig, but he did enjoy a full measure of satisfaction from the two sons with which he was blessed. R' Zelig called his first child Yissachar Dov. The name Yissachar reflected R' Zelig's fervent wish that he be a *talmid chacham* like the first Yissachar, son of Yaakov *Avinu*, of whom the Torah says: "Yissachar is a strong-boned donkey lying between the fields," on which Rashi comments: He bears the yoke of Torah like a strong donkey whom they load with a heavy burden. Dov had been the name of R' Zelig's saintly grandfather.

When R' Zelig's second son was born he called him Zevulun. Perhaps R' Zelig thought he would be like the first Zevulun who was blessed to give rise to a tribe of merchant princes, destined to support their brethren of Yissachar who would sit in their tents and learn Torah. R' Zelig never explained.

From early youth, the two differed. Yissachar Dov would retire to a corner, engrossed in learning; Zevulun, a little naughty but, nevertheless, much loved by friend and neighbor, would join with the other children in their many games. When they came of age and married, Yissachar Dov remained in the tents of Torah, while Zevulun, though he set aside time for learning, turned to the world of commerce and prospered greatly.

Yissachar Dov's righteous and valorous wife, Lipshe, eager to take upon herself the burden of supporting the family and free her husband from the need to leave his studies, opened a small grocery. Happiness filled the humble home of R' Yissachar Dov and Lipshe, and made up for their poverty. And blessing followed upon happiness; two sons were born to them.

But the sunny years came to an abrupt end. Lipshe died in the throes of childbirth. Her husband was left a widower, the little boys orphans. There was no woman at home; there were no means of support. R' Yissachar Dov's bright world had become bleak.

∻ And a Brother for Trouble Will Be Born
(*Mishlei* 17:17)

"I know, my brother, I know," said Zevulun to R' Yissachar Dov, "from the time that you were on your own you have refused to take anything, even a loan, from anyone, even from your own flesh and blood. When your dear wife, peace be with her, was alive, you never turned, or needed to turn, to another. But now your cup of suffering is full and I cannot stand by. I will not suggest charity. No! I will make you an offer. Let us make an agreement like that of the first Zevulun and Yissachar. You will sit and learn and I will support you and your children and we will both share your reward in the World-to-Come. Our holy Torah has sanctified such an arrangement. Does it not say: 'Rejoice Zevulun in your going out and Yissachar in your tents' (*Devarim* 33:18), and does it not even give precedence to Zevulun over Yissachar?"

R' Yissachar heard and was troubled. Should he treat Torah as a commodity to be bought and sold? In his trouble he turned to the *gaon*, R' Binyaminke, the *rav* of Volkovysk, the father of the *gaon*-to-be, R' Yehoshua Leib Diskin, *rav* of Brisk and later *Yerushalayim*.

R' Binyaminke was wise and honest, yet shrewd and clever. He listened to R' Yissachar Dov's doubts and fears. "Rest your mind," he said. "You will not in the least break your vow not to benefit from the labor of others, and you will not lose an iota of your share in the World-to-Come. Accept your brother's offer. When a candle is lit from another it does not diminish the light of the first. In the time of the *Mishnah* such a contract was made.

Azariah provided for his brother, Shimon, who sat and learned Torah; they agreed that Azariah would share in Shimon's reward."

R' Yissachar Dov was now at peace with himself. He would consent to the agreement on one condition. He wished to go up to the Holy Land, to Jerusalem, and learn Torah close to the site of the Temple. Would Zevulun be willing to supply passage to *Eretz Yisrael*? Zevulun was willing.

The agreement was properly written and signed. R' Yissachar Dov packed his belongings and he and his two sons went up to the Holy Land. There he lived in Jerusalem devoted to the learning of the Torah, while his brother sent him a monthly stipend, freeing him from the worries of a livelihood. R' Yissachar Dov lived in a world bounded by the four cubits of *halachah* and that little world was complete in itself.

But in 5665 (1905) war broke out between Russia and Japan. Travel was disrupted and postal service between Russia and *Eretz Yisrael* was nearly cut off. *Purim* had already passed and the money order, which Zevulun sent every month, or at most, every second month, was long overdue. R' Yissachar Dov became concerned. How would he pay the expenses of the fast-approaching *Pesach*? He refused to accept a loan from the free-loan society. Had he not taken it upon himself not to depend on the favors of others? Day followed day and in R' Yissachar Dov's home there was, as yet, no hint of the *Pesach*-to-be — no *shmurah matzah*, no wine for the four cups.

Not far from R' Yissachar Dov lived a very poor teacher, R' Lebel Karliner, who supported himself and his family with difficulty. His income was slight. But Zlata, R' Lebel's good wife, was an *eishes chayil*, a woman of valor, stretching the little that came in, far beyond its imaginable limits. During the week, she would set aside one penny after another. And *Shabbos* after

Shabbos, though their table would not groan beneath the weight of a sumptuous banquet, it managed to display fish and even modest portions of chicken.

Zlata had a secret treasure, two gold coins — napoleons they were called — which she had received as a wedding gift from her mother-in-law. They had been hidden, these many years, in the bookcase, out of sight from a covetous eye and out of reach of a curious hand.

Once *Purim* had passed, until after the burning of the *chametz* on the eve of *Pesach,* Jerusalem was seized by a flurry of activity. The woman became the commander-in-chief of the household. The kitchen was declared off limits to the men, whose pockets and cuffs were full of tiny particles of the now-detestable *chametz*. Pots and pans were meticulously scraped, scrubbed and polished. Entire wardrobes — both summer and winter wear — were hauled to the courtyard to be cleaned and aired. Even the children were drafted. They were to clean and inspect the *sefarim*, which in many a Jerusalem home lined shelf upon shelf, from floor to ceiling. Just as the task of washing and polishing was the exclusive domain of the women in the family, the airing of the books was reserved as the particular privilege of the young. They would remove each precious volume and spread it out, open to the winds, in the courtyard or on the flat roof. A stiff breeze, riffling the pages, would blow away any chance crumb that might have stolen in during a meal. It was a task which the children performed with much vigor and even more enthusiasm.

R' Lebel Karliner's two sons chose a day, early in *Nisan*, to air the *sefarim*. In the course of the work, little Nachumke's eye fell on two shiny coins, the two gold napoleons which his mother, Zlata, kept for 'whatever trouble that should not come.' Nachumke was fascinated. Never had he seen coins which

shone like this. No one was around; no one was looking. In one quick move he slipped the coins deep into his pocket.

It was, as we said, a day early in *Nisan.* R' Yissachar Dov had not yet received his usual stipend from abroad. He went to the Western Wall and poured out his heart before the Provider for all and begged Him not to put him, Yissachar Dov, to the test; to allow him to maintain his vow not to depend on others.

While returning home from the Wall, he chanced upon Nachumke, the little son of his neighbor R' Lebel Karliner. The youngster was playing with coins, rolling them across the smooth cobblestones. But what coins! To his amazement, when he drew near, he saw that the coins were two gold napoleons, a large sum for those days. A single one would be enough to support a family for a month. The mistaken thought flashed through R' Yissachar Dov's mind that his prayers had been answered. The thought blossomed into temptation; the tempta-tion gave fruit to false reasoning. Yes! Yes! In Heaven they had taken mercy upon him and sent him this windfall, a temporary 'loan' to prepare for the forthcoming *Pesach.* When the money order would arrive he would return the napoleons. R' Yissachar Dov could not resist the whisperings within himself.

"Nachumke, where did you get those coins?" he asked.

"I found them," answered the boy.

"And what are you going to do with them?"

"I'm going to buy candy from Senor Nissim. His stand is right nearby, not far from the Churva."

"And if in place of those two little coins I were to give you three or even four big ones, you could buy lots of candy. How would you like that?"

R' Yissachar Dov did not wait for the reply. He snatched the two napoleons from the youngster, thrust four *kabaks,* large in diameter but low in value, into his hand and marched off. His *yeitzer hara* was content.

Nachumke, smiling a smile of childish joy, turned the large coins over and over again in his hands. He then hurried off to Senor Nissim and, in return for the *kabaks,* he received a fistful of sugar candies as well as some packets of chocolate. Nachumke returned home in high spirits.

When R' Lebel Karliner's sons had finished airing and inspecting the *sefarim*, they returned them to the bookcase. Zlata came by to assure herself that her secret cache was undisturbed. But lo and behold! They were gone! A desperate cry burst forth from her throat, "The napoleons! Help! They have stolen my treasure!"

Nachumke paled to the sound and darted away. His sudden action aroused suspicion. R' Lebel seized him and held him by his little ear. With eyes blazing, he roared at him to reveal the whereabouts of the napoleons. The boy broke down in tears and told how he had come upon the coins and used them to buy candy from Senor Nissim who had a stand near the Churva of R' Yehudah HeChasid. R' Lebel went off like a whirlwind to Nissim and demanded that he immediately return the two napoleons. Nissim denied that he had ever received the gold coins. He emptied his money chest, containing the day's receipts, before R' Lebel's eyes. "Look and see for yourself," he said. "You will find *kabakim, bishlikim.* But napoleons? Never have I received a gold napoleon!"

R' Lebel's cries were heard throughout the alleys of the Old City. "Thief!" he screamed at Nissim. "How dare you cheat a little boy out of napoleons!" But Nissim defended himself vigorously, insisting that R' Lebel was trumping up a charge against him.

When R' Lebel saw that all his shouting was in vain, he took hold of Nissim by the collar and, in a commanding voice, ordered, "Let's be off to R' Shmuel. R' Shmuel will have something to say on the matter." Nissim packed his wares, folded his stand, slung them over his back and followed his tormentor to R' Shmuel Salant, the revered rabbi of Jerusalem. After a thorough investigation, R' Shmuel's *beis din* (court) handed down its verdict. Senor Nissim would have to swear that he had, indeed, not received two napoleons from Nachumke. A day after *Pesach,* when the vacation would be over and the *beis din* would once more be in session, was chosen for administering the oath. Nissim accepted the verdict calmly, at least on the surface.

The tale of the two napoleons was the talk of the town — on street corners, in *batei midrashos* and even in the *mikveh* in the basement of the Nisan Beck Synagogue. But none of the tumult reached R' Yissachar Dov's ears. After buying what he needed for *Pesach* with the two napoleons, he returned to his spot in the women's section of the Shoneh Halachos Synagogue on HaYehudim Street and took up his learning once more. Even when he went to the *mikveh* before *Shabbos*, he would do so early in the morning. He did not want to meet up with those who made it their haunt and enjoyed spending long hours there, spouting nonsense and not quite avoiding the questionable edges of idle gossip, *lashon hara*. Talk flew back and forth, but R' Yissachar heard not a word.

The bright days of *Pesach* passed. The stores on HaYehudim Street, which had been closed halfdays during *Chol HaMoed,* were, now, fully open once more, and Senor Nissim returned to his usual post near the Churva of R' Yehuda HeChasid. But he was no longer his old self. He remembered painfully that the day when he must swear the oath in the *beis din* of R' Shmuel was steadily approaching. Hour by hour the time grew shorter; hour by hour his countenance grew longer. If he was not to be numbered among the refined souls of Jerusalem, he, nevertheless, greatly feared uttering the Name, even though it was to the absolute truth.

In those days, when Senor Nissim had already resumed selling sweets, the postman knocked on R' Yissachar Dov's door. The long-awaited money order had arrived. R' Yissachar Dov hurriedly went to exchange it.

On his way home, he stopped by R' Lebel's and waited for the teacher to finish his lessons and dismiss his young charges. He then approached him and in a breaking voice told him his story of Nachumke and the two napoleons.

"Surely, R' Lebel," he said, "you understand, do you not, that I was not at all trying to take the napoleons from the boy. But, since Nachumke told me that he had found them and that he intended to buy sweets with them from Senor Nissim, and since I was in desperate straits, I felt that it would not be immoral to take the napoleons as a loan and return them after funds arrived from my brother in Russia. I succumbed to the whisperings of the *yeitzer hara*.

"I convinced myself that since the *halachah* states that what a child finds belongs to his father, the napoleons really belonged to you. And yet they were not really yours, I told myself. They had not reached your hand and you did not, as yet, have full legal possession. Since there was no true legal bar, I could take them temporarily. I did not act properly. Please forgive me, nevertheless, R' Lebel, for taking this loan without your knowledge."

R' Lebel smiled good-naturedly and said, "Had you asked me for the money as a loan until relief came, I would not have hesitated to give it to you. Certainly, I forgive you and am happy that, even without my intending to do so, you used my money to celebrate *Pesach* with joy. However, we have another more serious problem. An honest Jew has been suspected, through no fault of his own, of taking the napoleons from the boy in exchange for a few candies."

When Yissachar Dov heard that without meaning to he had cast suspicion onto poor Senor Nissim, he was horrified. He half-ran, half-strode to Nissim's candy stand and, like a guilty child, confessed that it was he who had caused him all the shame and suffering and that he would do anything to gain his forgiveness.

But none of R' Yissachar Dov's entreaties moved Senor Nissim. He was thankful that Heaven had spared him the ordeal of swearing the oath, and that his innocence had come to light to confound all the slanderers and scoffers who had spilled his soul's blood, as it were. Yet, suffering of body and spirit had been his lot in the last weeks. He could not simply forgive and forget.

R' Yissachar Dov burst into bitter tears; his world was being destroyed about him. The tears softened Nissim's stubbornness and he said, "I will forgive you, but on one condition. I have heard that you are a great *tzaddik*, and the *chacham* of our synagogue always tells us that it is written that a *tzaddik* decrees and the Holy One fulfills those decrees. To this day, I have not been blessed with a son, only daughters, and I feel that my life is not yet a life since I do not have anyone who will say *Kaddish* for me. If you will promise me that I will be granted a son, all is forgiven, all is pardoned."

R' Yissachar Dov heard the condition and was even more dispirited. "Senor Nissim," he said, "how can you ask of a Jew, who fell into temptation and whose sins are always before his eyes, that which even Yaakov *Avinu* was unable to promise Rachel *Imeinu*? But, the gates of prayer are not locked and he who forgives his neighbor deserves to have the Holy One favor him and grant him his heart's desire."

Nissim chose to see R' Yissachar Dov's words as a promise and said, "You are forgiven! You are forgiven! And I would like you to be the *sandak* for the son who will be born to us with the help of *Hashem*."

Senor Nissim was not to be disappointed. A year later, all Maidan Square thrilled to the news that, after five daughters, his wife Serena had given birth to a son.

On the night before the *bris*, the *chachamim* of Yeshivath Porath Yosef gathered and sang *zemiros*, offered up prayers of praise and read passages of *Zohar*, all to help guard and protect the mother and the tender infant from harm. Senor Nissim waited on them and took care that there should be no lack of wine which gladdens the heart. The next day a splendid *bris* was arranged. All the rabbis and *chachamim* of the Ashkenazic and Sephardic communities arrived. You could almost touch the joy with your fingers. But no one could fathom why the Ashkenazi, R' Yissachar Dov, was chosen to be given the honor of *sandak* for a baby who was pure Sephardi.

But you and I, dear readers, we know.

A Wise Man Is Better than a Prophet

I t was a hot summer day at the end of *Tammuz* 5665 (1905). The Rishon L'Zion of Jerusalem, the Chacham Bashi, Yaakov Shaul Elyashar, was dozing in his armchair. Extreme age and many years of suffering from heart disease had taken their toll. He was growing weaker and weaker and the state of his health gave rise to anxiety among the members of his community, the Sephardic Jews, whose shepherd he was.

But in contrast to his physical condition his mind was clear and settled — age often treats *talmidei chachamim* well in that respect. And he managed the communal affairs from his residence in the Even Yisrael quarter on the Yaffo Road. Nothing was done without first consulting him.

A sharp knock was heard at the door. When R' Aharon Sostial, the trusty *shammash* of the Rishon L'Zion opened it, a clerk of the Turkish Post Office handed him a telegram sent from the main post office of Warsaw, Poland. It was addressed to the Rishon L'Zion, HaRav Yaakov Shaul Elyashar. It was surprisingly long and attached to it was a receipt stating that the sender had already paid in advance for the response which it requested. R' Chaim Michel Michlin, the personal secretary to the Rishon L'Zion, read the telegram to him. It was in Hebrew but written in Latin characters and contained the following:

Warsaw, 13 July 1905.

I, the *rav* of Novominsk, in the name of the entire Jewish community, request your aid in an urgent matter. A few months ago a government official was murdered here. The brothers, Noach and Eliezer Horowitz, and the woman, Mattl, who are now to be found in Jerusalem in the home of Yitzchak Friedman of Mezeritch, testified falsely in the case before they left. Out of hatred, they bore witness against five Christians who, on the basis of their testimony, were found guilty of murder and sentenced to death. We request that his honor examine Noach and Eliezer Horowitz, and the woman, Mattl, thoroughly, and have them admit that they gave false testimony against the Christians. If we save the condemned, the Jews will avoid disgrace, hatred, and pogrom. Please notify the Russian consul in Jerusalem to relay your findings to the authorities in Russia.

Signed:

Rabbiner Rabinovitz,
Novominsk, District of Warsaw

The Rishon L'Zion was perplexed. It seemed odd that the governmental postal service in Poland would allow the transmission of a telegram which was aimed at upsetting officially given testimony. Who was wise enough to read between the lines of this strange request? After a protracted silence, he turned to R' Chaim Michel and said, "We must first find and speak to the people named. The picture will then be clearer. Please go and meet with them."

R' Chaim Michel left and made his way to the address specified in the telegram. The two men and the woman gave the impression of being simple folk, uneducated and quite humble. The men were shoemakers by trade. R' Chaim Michel did not tell them about the telegram, but struck up a conversation with them and turned the talk to the story of the killing of the government official. They were surprised that he knew about the matter and viewed him with suspicion. And, simple as they were, they guarded their tongues and refused to discuss the subject. When R' Chaim Michel suggested they change their place of residence lest they come under the eye of the Russian consulate (Poland was ruled at the time by Russia) and the local police, he gained their confidence. They then told him of the background which led up to the murder and gave all the details.

It was clear that the five Christians had indeed taken part in the murder. The official had been cruel and had brought suffering to many. A number of Jews had given aid to the killers because the official had been a vicious Jew-hater, but the killing itself had been carried out by the five Christians. The three expressed alarm at the death sentence. They feared that it could trigger a pogrom against the Jews, for there were a number of non-Jews who were aware that Jews had been involved in the plot and now, it was only the Christians who had been sentenced to death.

R' Chaim Michel returned and reported to the Chacham Bashi. R' Yaakov Shaul realized that they were dealing with a matter of utmost importance. He turned to those about him and said, "Do you not see that I am too weak to deal with such a matter? Let us convene the leaders of the community for an urgent meeting. Perhaps we will arrive at a solution. 'Salvation comes through the advice of many' (*Mishlei* 24:6). Go and arrange for their assembly."

R' Chaim Michel drew up a list; R' Aharon Sostial hurried out to inform the communal leaders.

On Thursday evening, 26 *Tammuz* 5665 (1905), some twenty men of the Sephardi community gathered together in answer to the summons of the Rishon L'Zion. The session began after the *Maariv* prayers and were presided over by the Chacham Bashi, sunken in his armchair. R' Chaim Michel read aloud the telegram and told of his meeting with the people. There was a heated discussion, various opinions were voiced and finally, after a long argument over each and every word, a reply, which was found agreeable to all, was drafted.

The Chacham Bashi had not entered the discussion. He would dip into his gold snuffbox from time to time for a pinch of snuff — a sure sign of his deep concentration. When the final draft was read aloud, he rose from his seat with difficulty and spoke, "Dear brothers, I have listened carefully to all that has been said. With all due respect, I do not agree with a single word uttered. In my opinion, you have all erred. I believe that the telegram was sent by the families of the condemned, and they have paid for the reply in advance, in an attempt to save the murderers from their fate. If we carry out their request and have the witnesses deny their testimony, this will stir up the darkest passions of the enemies of Israel. We are liable to bring, *chas veshalom*, great tragedy to the Jewish communities in Poland."

Those assembled there were amazed and asked the *rav* what should be a fitting reply.

After a short pause, he said, "If we were to avoid an answer completely, all the better. However, the reply is already paid for and etiquette demands that we respond. I suggest that we say that in my capacity as a *rav* in an area which is under the rule and protection of the sovereign government of Turkey, I am forbidden to involve myself and intervene in the internal affairs of another state. Such an answer is noncommittal. It says nothing good or bad, nor will it complicate the issue."

Not all concurred with the Chacham Bashi and the argument resumed.

The Rishon L'Zion turned to his secretary and said, "My dear R' Chaim Michel, I want you and my *shammash* to go immediately, in spite of the late hour, to R' Shmuel Salant in the Churva of R' Yehudah HeChasid. Wake him up and tell him the whole story. Do not give him my opinion nor that of the others. Follow his advice, no matter what he says. Do not return here; there is no time to lose. Here is my official seal; affix it to the reply which R' Shmuel will draft."

The decision of the Chacham Bashi to refer the matter to R' Shmuel Salant won unanimous approval.

R' Shmuel was accustomed to eat a small meal after *Maariv* and retire until midnight. He would then awake and learn until the morning. The Chacham Bashi's secretary and *shammash* would have to disturb the elderly *gaon's* short nap. However, they had no choice. The Chacham Bashi had insisted that the reply could not await the morrow. R' Aharon Sostial, a tall, powerful man, carried a lamp and lit the way for himself and his companion through the streets of a darkened Jerusalem. They reached R' Shmuel Salant's home. R' Chaim Michel knocked lightly on the door and the elderly rabbi asked, "Who's there?"

Upon being told, he said, "Ah, R' Chaim Michel, my friend, at so late an hour? What has happened?"

The secretary begged his pardon and replied, "We have an urgent matter at hand." R' Shmuel, who had become blind with age, felt his way to the door, opened it and invited them in. "What is all the trouble about?" he asked.

He heard them out and listened to the telegram as it was read to him. He asked that it be read once more, and then once again. "And what is the opinion of my friend and colleague Rav Elyashar?" asked R' Shmuel.

"There was a disagreement between the Chacham Bashi and some of the heads of the community who gathered in his home to discuss the matter. They decided to refer the decision to your honor."

The venerable rabbi rested his forehead on an arm, in concentrated thought. After a moment he said, "The cost of the telegram and the prepaid reply must be at least two hundred and fifty rubles — a considerable sum. I believe that it was sent by the families of the condemned. They would be the most likely to lay out such monies. I think the telegram is fraudulent and the Rav of Novominsk, if such a *rav* exists at all, knows nothing of it."

"And, in the Rav's opinion, what shall we reply?"

"Nothing, in effect. For example you can say that I and the Chacham Bashi serve as rabbis in a country which is under the protection and rule of Turkey and are forbidden to intervene in the internal affairs of another state."

It was as if *ruach hakodesh* (Divine Spirit) had spoken from the throats of the two old *tzaddikim*, who, without having uttered a word to each other, gave voice to identical advice. R' Chaim Michel immediately, following their instructions, sent off a telegram to Novominsk that very night.

This had all occurred on a Thursday. A mere two days later, on *Shabbos* afternoon, the Chacham Bashi returned his soul — old and full of days — to his Creator. He was ninety-two years of age and his mind had been clear to the very end. He had been right. There had not been too much time to spare.

The following item appeared in *Hazman*, printed in Russia, and it was also printed in *Hatzfirah*, in Warsaw:

Thanks to the keenness of Jerusalem's rabbis, our enemies did not catch us in their net with the false telegram which they sent in the name of the Rav of Novominsk, and we were thus saved from riots and pogroms. If they had been led astray, there would have been no limit to what we would have suffered.

The rabbis had, indeed, divined the truth. Have our Sages not said: "A wise man is better than a prophet"?

Measure for Measure

The road from Tel-Aviv sweeps in dizzying curves as it approaches Jerusalem, and when the traveler is almost upon the city, he comes almost face to face with a small well-kept lawn on the hill ahead. Its centerpiece is made up of bushes clipped to form the warm Hebrew welcome: *"Beruchim Habaim LeYerushalayim* — blessed are you who come to Jerusalem." The road straightens out; there is a traffic light and then, on the right, a row of twisted olive trees in somber green lines the way. Behind them on a low rise, stand buildings faced in the cream-colored Jerusalem stone, now somewhat dingy with age. The traveler has arrived.

So it is today. But, less than a generation ago, two fine institutions stood at Jerusalem's entrance, framing it like doorposts — the United Old-Age Home, and across the road, the Ezrat Nashim Hospital. Now, not far from the foot of Yaffo Road the Egged Bus Terminal occupies the site of the old-age home and facing it is the original building of the hospital, worn and neglected, seemingly marking time, as if waiting to be replaced by a modern skyscraper.

On either side of its cast-iron gate, at the entrance of the old-age home, stood two backless benches where the old would sit, men on the right, women on the left, stooped and weary, staring listlessly at the traffic and the people who passed them by without a glance.

They all seemed alike, dim eyed and sad, as if the spark of life had left them, never to return. But on closer examination, one could distinguish, from among them, one elderly Jew sitting at the far edge of the men's bench. He looked different with his erect posture and piercing stare. He seemed to look life full in the face and not dwell only on the past.

His name was R' Berel Zlodovitz, originally of Minsk, Russia, where he and his brother, Baruch David, had owned sugar factories and other large properties.

R' Berel had been both wealthy and generous with a well-deserved reputation for his wise distribution of charity. His hand had been open for anyone who sought help and, especially so, for the poor of Jerusalem. He had sent them large sums of money twice a year, to tide them through the Festivals. He and his family had purchased land where the Kollel Minsk built free housing for its scholars and their families.

In Minsk, R' Berel rose early every day and prayed with a sunrise *minyan* of *vasikin*. A quick breakfast and he was off to his factory. He was determined to arrive before his workers to make sure that everything was in its place, that each worker arrived on time and that he took up his proper station. The workers all knew of R' Berel's near-worship of punctuality and woe to the man who came late.

One morning, R' Berel rose early and prayed with the *vasikin*, as usual, finished his breakfast and began to make his way to the factory. A tearful old Jew pounced upon him midway and said, "Reb Yid, do me a true favor. Be the tenth man; I need a *minyan*. Today is my mother's *yahrzeit* and I have never missed a *Kaddish* for her in all my life."

R' Berel hesitated. How could he come late to work? Who would check to see that the hundreds of workers in his plant arrived precisely on time? Yet, his kind heart could not resist the appeal of a Jew who wished to say *Kaddish* for his mother. R' Berel wavered for a moment, this way and that, and followed the old man.

He stepped into the nearby *shul*. To his amazement, he was not the *tenth*; he and the old man were but the first two; not another soul was in the *shul*. His heart boiled over with anger. "Why did you fool me?" he shouted. "Why did you steal my precious time? I'm no idler! Do you know that I have hundreds of workers whom I must supervise? I must make sure that they do their work properly. I'm leaving!"

"I'm not going to let you budge from here!" said the old Jew. "I swore to my mother, before her death, that I would never miss a *Kaddish* during the first year or on her *yahrzeit*. And now, what with this state of emergency, while the Czar's forces fight the Communists, it is almost impossible to gather a *minyan*. No, I cannot let you leave until I say *Kaddish* with a *minyan*."

"And what of my hundreds of workers who await my orders in my big factory?" demanded R' Berel.

"Not a thing will happen. Each one knows his place and his job without your standing over him. Besides, for whom are you working so hard? In another day or two, or perhaps a week or two, the Bolsheviks will be victorious. They'll seize your factory and everything you own. However, no power in the world can take away this *mitzvah*, this act of kindness which I ask of you; it will be preserved for you forever into the next world."

"What do you mean 'they'll take everything'? Is it theirs? Didn't I sweat and toil with my two hands all my life to build it up? By what right can they take away the fruits of my labor?" screamed R' Berel.

But none of R' Berel's arguments and protests helped, in the least. He bit his lips and stayed put until the determined man assembled his *minyan*, recited a few chapters of *Tehillim* and said his *Kaddish*.

Like a bird freed from its cage, R' Berel flew from his clutches and ran as fast and furiously as he could towards his factory, glancing nervously, from time to time, at his gold watch.

When he was a few hundred yards from his goal, he saw his foreman running towards him waving his arms, motioning him to stop. He approached R' Berel and cried, "Run for your life! The Bolsheviks have seized the plant and they're looking for you. Go wherever your legs will carry you and hide from the murderers!"

R' Berel and his wife hid in a cellar and evaded the claws of the revolutionaries. Subsequently they fled Russia.

At the end of World War I, R' Berel and his wife decided that the Diaspora held nothing more for them. They packed their few belongings and made their way up to *Eretz Yisrael*. The great philanthropist of Minsk reached Jerusalem penniless, with barely more than the shirt on his back.

The people of Jerusalem were not ungrateful. They remembered the kindness of their former benefactor and received R'

Berel and his wife with honor. The *gabbaim* and directors of the various institutions which had enjoyed his favors in the past gathered a special fund for R' Berel to put him back on his feet. They were willing to give him a loan to set up a sugar factory or any enterprise he saw fit.

R' Berel politely rejected all offers. After all he had gone through, he felt that it was not worthwhile to invest time and effort to acquire wealth, which is here today and gone tomorrow. He had spent long years in heaping up the goods of this world, only to suffer disillusionment and heartache. Now, he decided to devote the rest of his days to the study of Torah and the fulfillment of good deeds.

The new building of the United Old-Age Home had been erected through R' Berel's personal donation. The directors offered R' Berel the use of a wing as a home for himself and his wife. R' Berel accepted. And so it was, that R' Berel, who in his heyday had been called the Rothschild of Russia, became one of the residents of the Jerusalem old-age home, along with the poorest and humblest of the city.

R' Berel and his wife soon grew accustomed to their new surroundings and became beloved by their fellow residents and the staff. Nor did the heads of Jerusalem's institutions neglect him. They visited him frequently.

A particularly close friendship developed between R' Berel and R' Yechiel Michel Tucatzinsky, the head of the Eitz Chaim Yeshivah and its institutions in the Machaneh Yehudah section of Jerusalem. R' Michel lived nearby in the Eitz Chaim neighborhood which R' Berel had helped build and R' Berel and his wife became frequent guests at his *Shabbos* and *Yom Tov* table.

One year, on the morning of *Hoshana Rabbah* after *Shacharis*, R' Michel came by to wish R' Berel the customary blessing of a good year and a *piska tava* (literally, a good note; the last-minute recommendations received in Heaven on *Hoshana Rabbah* marking the end of the year of judgment).

R' Michel entered the little *succah* built by the old-age home especially for R' Berel and found him in exceptionally good humor.

"*Gut Moed*, R' Michel!" said R' Berel. "Good news! This year I have earned a *piska tava*; it is not meant for this world but for the World-to-Come! Sit down, R' Michel; make a *brachah*, a *leisheiv basuccah,* and I'll explain."

Now, R' Berel had a strange habit which seemed to run completely counter to his nature. Although he firmly refused any offer of assistance, he would nevertheless beg a cigarette from any passing smoker. This amazed everyone for since it was well known that R' Berel still enjoyed a smoke, his friends would always leave a few packages of good-quality cigarettes when they came by for a visit. It was also surprising that no one ever refused the request of the elderly man.

R' Berel was about to solve the mystery.

"We are all aware," said R' Berel, "that the Communist Revolution was not a matter of coincidence. G-d judges justly! I feel that this came about as punishment for exploitation of the workers. We refused to see that every man is cast in the Divine image, *betzelem Elokim,* and we did not give each man his due respect. I, too, am guilty.

"I owned a sugar factory, perhaps the largest one in Russia. Even though I was generous and courteous to my workers, nevertheless, in terms of work, I was the most exacting of employers. Even though I had many things to attend to, I would arrive at the plant a quarter of an hour before the beginning of the workday and, from my office door, I would watch each worker as he entered. I had foremen, but I insisted on having an eye on everything. And Heaven help the worker who neglected his duties when I was around.

"One day, a middle-aged Jew named Feivel did not show up at the beginning of the day. I kept looking at my watch. Finally, at nine-thirty, Feivel rushed in, all out of breath, and ran to the boiling vat, an hour and a half late. I was furious! I shot out of my armchair, flew over and grabbed him by the collar.

" 'Feivke!' I said angrily, 'What is this all about?' I pointed accusingly at the hands of my gold watch.

" 'Oh, R' Berel,' he replied, 'I wanted to go into your office and apologize for my coming late, but I was afraid to. My wife's in bed after surgery and several of the children are burning up with fever. Early in the morning my wife didn't feel well at all, and I went to fetch a doctor; that is why I am late.' His whole body shook with fear as he spoke.

"I was cold as ice and dismissed him with, 'Your wife should be sick at your expense, not mine.'

"Poor Feivke was very upset by my words; he cried at his work. I was proud of my ruthless forcefulness. I calmly returned, at peace with myself, to my comfortable office and armchair.

"When the Bolsheviks seized my property, I was forced to hide in a cellar in fear for my life. I had time to think of my behavior and remembered spilling poor Feivke's blood, so to speak. The Holy One, Blessed is He, was repaying me in kind for my mistreatment of Feivke and his fellows.

"I always prayed that the Holy One would pardon me for that sin; it remained on my soul like an indelible sin. I took it upon myself to beg for cigarettes; each time I would reach out and beg, my heart cringed in pain and shame. But it was not a sufficient penance for the humiliation of a poor Jew crushed by afflictions. For, every time I stretched out my hand, I did not meet a refusal. Instead I would meet a generous response and

receive warm words of comfort which rescued me from total humility. I have continually worried, lest I leave this world with this sin of shaming an unfortunate still on my soul.

"But yesterday I stretched out my hand and said to a passing smoker, 'Reb Yid, if you might be so good, could you spare a cigarette?'

"He pushed me off and said, 'You should smoke at your expense, not mine.'

"At that moment, I knew I had been forgiven. From now on, I can look quietly and with a pure heart towards the day I will take leave from this world for the World-That-Is-All-Good. This is my *piska tava*."

That year, full of days and hardship, R' Berel passed on to the World-of-Truth. Jerusalem showed him great honor; his bier was borne on the shoulders of pallbearers from the old-age home at the entrance of the city all the way to the heights of *Har Hazeisim*, the Mount of Olives.

This volume is part of
THE ARTSCROLL SERIES®
an ongoing project of
translations, commentaries and expositions
on Scripture, Mishnah, liturgy, history,
the classic Rabbinic Writings,
biographies, and thought.

For a brochure of current publications
visit your local Hebrew bookseller
or contact the publisher:

Mesorah Publications, Ltd.

4401 Second Avenue
Brooklyn, New York 11232
(718) 921-9000